ABOUT THE AUTHOR

George G. Gilman was born in 1936 in what
was then a small village east of London. He
attended local schools until the age of fifteen.
Upon leaving school he abandoned all earlier
ambitions and decided to become a
professional writer, with strong leanings
towards the mystery novel. He wrote short
stories and books during evenings, lunch
hours, at weekends, and on the time of
various employers while he worked for an
international newsagency, a film company, a
weekly book-trade magazine and the Royal
Air Force.

His first short (love) story was published
when he was sixteen and the first (mystery)
novel ten years later. He has been a full-time
writer since 1970, writing mostly Westerns
which have been translated into a dozen
languages and have sold in excess of 16
million copies. He is married and lives on the
Dorset coast, which is as far west as he
intends to move right now.

The Breed Woman

George G. Gilman

NEW ENGLISH LIBRARY
Hodder and Stoughton

for
I. L.
who regularly provides
the stake.

Copyright © 1989 by
George G. Gilman

First published in
Great Britain in 1989
by New English
Library Paperbacks

An NEL paperback
original

British Library C.I.P.

Gilman, George G., *1936–*
The breed woman.
I. Title   II. Series
823'.914[F]

ISBN 0-450-49365-2

Printed and bound in Great
Britain for Hodder and Stoughton
Paperbacks, a division of Hodder
and Stoughton Ltd., Mill Road,
Dunton Green, Sevenoaks, Kent
TN13 2YA (Editorial Office: 47
Bedford Square, London, WC1B
3DP) by Richard Clay,
Bungay, Suffolk.

1

The beans were hard, half cooked and on the cool side. And the bacon was tough and stringy, off a hog that had lived longer than the average for its kind. But the beer served up in the saloon was the best Edge had tasted for many miles. So he figured he did not have much cause for complaint in a place like the Golden Eagle, and he did not complain.

Supper was more in keeping with his surroundings than the beer. The Golden Eagle was a pretty good match for the town of which it was a part.

Ross was a small two-street community on a gentle slope in the foothills of the Klamath Mountains in south western Oregon, north of the California line. Gold Rush country thirty years earlier, but timber land now. The gold had not lasted long enough for Ross ever to be a boom town and those few grubbers who got lucky had either frittered away their new-found wealth on transitory pleasures or hogged it and moved on. The wealth which was spent in Ross had not been used to make the town a better place in which to live.

More recently the timber company owners and their workers now made up the majority of the town's population; but they, likewise, were not inclined to take any pride in Ross.

Which Edge thought he could understand. Because some day pretty soon, the timber in the vicinity would all be felled and there would be no need of a town here. Be it beautiful to look at or just a huddle of crudely-built, worse-for-wear shacks of varying sizes where a man, woman or family could eat, sleep and shelter from the worst of the north country weather and purchase the essentials of life or a few scant luxuries.

As Edge neared the end of the supper that eased his hunger

7

but gave him no pleasure, he found himself reflecting that the stock in trade of the Golden Eagle Saloon was probably not considered a luxury in a town like Ross. That at the end of the day, a working man around here felt a compelling need to take a drink before he bedded down. To erase from his mind the knowledge that his existence was comprised so largely of work for work's sake. A man with sufficient alcohol inside him might be able to blot out what had taken place during the day just over, sink into a deep sleep and gather strength for the next day's work. Instead of tossing and turning, restlessly awake during the night hours while he wondered just what the hell he was doing with his life.

'You ate it all up?' Paul Calhern said.

When Edge looked around at the man who interrupted his train of dark thoughts, he saw an expression close to incredulity on the darkly-bristled, prominently-jowled face of the owner of the Golden Eagle Saloon; five and a half feet tall, more than two hundred pounds in weight, and forty years old.

'Uh?' the half-breed grunted, and as soon as the implied query was out the substance of what the fat man had said registered in his mind.

'It surprises me you ate it all.'

The leather-aproned Calhern picked up the empty plate in one big and soft, unclean hand and the eating implements in the other as the expression of his square-shaped face with small eyes and fleshy lips altered to doleful disinterest. Which was how the saloonkeeper usually viewed the world between brief intervals of pretended interest in the subject of any brief exchanges in which he took a part.

It was just an hour ago that Edge became the fifth customer in the saloon. And in that time had learned from Calhern, without asking, the potted history of Ross: seen enough of the man to decide he was at one with his place and the town. Disenchanted and apathetic, but prepared to go through the motions of acting friendly if there was material gain to be made out of the effort.

'I was hungry,' Edge told him, delved into a shirt pocket for the makings.

8

'That'll do it,' Calhern allowed and looked down at the empty plate. Then he shook his head, not in disbelief this time: more like somebody who regrets the pain he has accidentally caused another. 'I told you the wife, who usually does the cookin', is——'

'She's visiting with her sick mother in Medford,' Edge broke in on the excuse as the batwing doors swung open and a man entered. 'You don't do the cooking as a general rule, but you did your best and——'

His voice trailed away when he saw that the saloonkeeper had lost interest in this subject they had already covered: then turned and waddled over to go behind his bar counter as the newcomer responded without enthusiasm to the greetings offered by three of the four men who played poker in a rear corner.

'Hiya, Eddie. You want your usual, I guess?' There was enforced cheerfulness in Calhern's tone which did not completely mask the fat man's uneasiness.

'Don't I always?' Eddie answered sourly. 'Which is why it's my friggin' usual, right?'

'Sure thing, Eddie.'

Calhern clattered the plate down, then dropped the cutlery to the floor in his hurry to serve the man. Who was in his mid-thirties, tall and powerfully built with a bushy black moustache that looked like it was carefully shaped to emphasise the implied toughness of his jutting jaw and deep-set, brooding eyes.

Eddie, who was dressed in denim pants held up by an ornately buckled belt and a garishly checked shirt, stood with his flat belly pressed up against the counter, hands splayed on the top, his back to the room until Calhern delivered a glass of beer and a shot of rye to him. Then he grasped a glass in each gnarled hand, threw the whiskey down in one and took a swallow that sank half the beer. Next he put the empty shot glass down on the counter, nodded for the waiting Calhern to refill it, and belched loudly.

All of this was done with a kind of studied intent that suggested that he was engaged in a ritual that never varied from

9

night to night as soon as he entered the Golden Eagle. Likewise, there was a stilted, over-rehearsed quality about the way he finished the beer, placed this empty glass down on the bar for Calhern to refill, then turned to rake a scornful and almost insolent stare over the small saloon with two of its half dozen tables occupied, in opposite corners of the room.

Three of the four card players met his contemptuous gaze fleetingly and looked away. Edge, carefully rolling a cigarette, returned the man's attention with an equal degree of frost: which caused Eddie to twist his mouthline into a more pronounced scowl before he ran the back of a hand across his moustache, wiped off beer foam.

'Ain't nothin' much in tonight?' Eddie said as he turned to belly up to the bar again. And timed a pause to let the words add up to an insult if that was how anybody chose to hear them, before he added: 'In the way of business for you?'

'There are the two passin'-through strangers, Eddie,' Calhern replied as he delivered the refilled beer glass. 'Makes it a kinda unusual evenin', I guess.'

'Whoopee!' Eddie growled in a parody of how the expression was supposed to sound. 'Two strangers breeze into Ross and we're meant to figure that's somethin' to celebrate.'

Calhern shrugged his fleshy shoulders and stooped to pick up the fallen knife and fork, took them with the dirty plate to the far end of counter where there was a basin of water.

The card game continued in the same quiet way as it had been played since Edge came into the Golden Eagle.

The half-breed struck a match on the underside of the table, lit his cigarette.

Eddie remained facing the bar, the glass of rye in one hand, beer in the other. Stood as rigid as a statue for a few moments, then began to drink in the same deliberate way he had done everything since he entered the saloon. First he sipped the whiskey, then took a larger swallow of the beer: left an unvarying interval of about ten seconds between each double drink.

Edge figured him for the local blowhard bully who might or might not raise a little hell, depending on what kind of day it had been for him and how the booze settled in his stomach. He arrived at this decision in the same way he had catalogued so much else about the town, the saloon and the men in here when he entered: as a mental exercise to keep his mind occupied, unable to dwell on other lines of thought that had no appeal for him but were irritatingly insistent.

In fact, it did not matter what kind of town this was. So long as it had a place where he could get something to eat and a glass of good beer, maybe a shot or two of whiskey that would not take the skin off the inside of his throat on the way down. Somewhere to bed down for the night. A livery where he could arrange for feed and water and shelter for his horse...

Though it did not really matter if there were none of these requirements in Ross, for he was either self-sufficient or the lush Oregon country could provide what he lacked if need be.

But, after a long ride of several weeks out of winter and into spring over the Cascade Mountains he felt a few of the creature comforts would not come amiss. So he was pleased to discover the Washington Livery Stable and the Grogan boarding house were both adequate for his purpose. Likewise the saloon. And Joel Washington, the Grogans and Paul Calhern were reasonably eager to provide for the requirements of this hard-looking but quiet-talking man who was the second stranger to come to Ross today.

The first was named Vincent Mitchell, sent to the Golden Eagle by Maud Grogan, now one of the players in the poker game that was underway when Edge entered the saloon. Mrs Grogan cooked breakfast for her roomers, but no other meals. That was the province of the Calherns: although Peggy Calhern was off visiting her sick mother in Medford and Mrs Grogan could not speak for the cooking skills of her husband.

While Edge had sipped a first glass of the good beer and waited to find out what kind of cook Paul Calhern was, he watched the poker game: ignored by all four players after three of them had greeted him, one of them invited him to take a hand. Vincent Mitchell, whose stylish mode of dress marked him out as the stranger among the others in their hard-wearing working clothes, had not offered a greeting to the half-breed.

And outside of the laconic monosyllables that are all a poker player needs to voice, he spoke just once within Edge's hearing: a sour-toned objection to the invitation after the half-breed declined to take a chair at the table.

'Four is fine for five card draw. Five is one too many, so it ain't. Nothing personal, mister?'

Edge had nodded he did not take the objection personally, then had begun his indifferent watch on the game across the room while he sipped the beer, waited for the food to be cooked and managed to cure his hunger with it.

And pondered his present surroundings, the people who gave it whatever kind of life it had. Which train of thought was little more edifying but a whole lot less irritating than notions about the kind of life he had chosen to live, and where it had gotten him!

First there was the dour-faced but eager-to-please liveryman, Joel Washington, 'just like the first president, mister, but my folks never claimed no direct line from good old George'. Then the garrulous Maud Grogan and her agitated husband Ray, who did a lot of wan smiling and bobbed his head a great deal, spoke fast whenever he talked like he was anxious to get said what he needed to before his wife cut him off in mid-flow.

The mostly unsmiling people he saw on the streets when he rode into this unprepossessing town of a couple of hundred citizens, walked between the livery and the boarding house, the boarding house and the saloon: some of whom were too preoccupied to notice him, a few who nodded curtly or even offered a terse greeting, most who pointedly ignored him.

Then Paul Calhern, who knew the secrets of keeping beer in fine condition but could not cook worth a damn. The three local lumber company men—either retired clerks or on light duty suitable to their age, he guessed—who accepted Edge's presence in Ross with equanimity.

Vincent Mitchell who seemed to be the kind of inveterate gambler who cared for nothing outside the game which presently engaged his attention. Had strong feelings only about the ground rules of such a game, one of which held there should be no more than four players in the game. Thus, Edge decided as he dropped the cigarette butt to the floor, crushed out its glowing embers under a boot heel, if one of the other players withdrew, Mitchell would have no objection to Edge replacing him.

Or the sour-tempered, taciturn Eddie who continued to stand at the bar, gazing into space and drinking beer and whiskey with unvarying intervals between. Of the people Edge had come across since he rode into Ross, Eddie was the odd man out. And yet paradoxically, he was more like the kind the half-breed would have thought would be in the majority in this grim timber town. Hard, narrow minded and not kindly disposed to strangers—especially the kind of stranger that Edge was.

Because Edge was himself hard, suspicious of strangers and ... well, maybe he wasn't narrow minded, but he had certainly gotten to nurture some fixed ideas lately! Like the way, damnit, he elected to spend his life among strangers he viewed with mistrust as he drifted from one frontier town to another, striving never to ride the same trail twice.

But it was getting time to change!

He was pushing fifty, which showed with every line engraved by time and experience into his leather-textured face, along with the world-weary expression of impassivity that seldom left the features shaded and shaped by the mixed parentage of a Scandinavian mother and a Mexican father.

The skin was deeply burnished, although outdoor living had shaded it darker than Latin heritage had coloured it at the outset. The black coloration of his hair, streaked with grey now, which hung long enough to brush his shoulders, and the basic bone structure of his face also came from his father's side.

The predominant physical feature drawn from his mother were his eyes: pale blue and permanently narrowed, which surveyed his surroundings with a brooding coolness that implied total lack of interest in what they saw, yet at the same time warned that they missed no detail of any consequence.

He clothed his six feet two inch, two hundred pound frame to suit the kind of life he led, in a hard-wearing, dark-hued outfit that had been much worn and was stained and dirtied by many miles on the trail and more rough sleeping than the kind of less than luxurious comfort that would be his tonight at the Grogan boarding house. Alone of the men in the saloon this evening, he carried a visible gun: a Frontier Colt that jutted from the holster tied down to his right thigh.

He was the way he was, did nothing for effect either in the style of his garb or, like Eddie, in his manner. So it was a matter of being the kind he was that caused him, more often than not, to arouse feelings of resentment, unease, even anger caused by fear, among people he came across in towns like Ross.

Whereas Vincent Mitchell would be generally more welcomed most places he went. For the pattern of the drifter into which he fitted was more acceptable, less provoking to ordinary working men and their womenfolk in frontier towns.

He was about the same age as Edge, an inch or so shorter but still tall. They weighed about the same, but there were some sagging bulges of flabby fat on the body of Mitchell, whose pale face had a dissipated look, like he was accustomed to enjoying the good life to excess when the cards were kind enough for him to cover the expense of high living.

He did not look at all hard, except on that occasion when he remarked on how he liked to play poker. Then there had been a just discernible gleam in his eyes for part of a second that suggested he could get vicious if he were pushed too far.

But in normal circumstances, it was unlikely that people who gave him no more than a passing glance would see any such signs of the darker side of the man's character. And in towns like Ross, few would see beyond his dudish, city-style mode of dress, the present threadbare condition of his three-piece suit suggesting the cards had not been running for him lately.

Discount the build of the man, but register his dudish ways, his liking for gambling and the menacing capacity for viciousness that lurked under the outer shell, and Vincent Mitchell reminded Edge of Adam Steele, Goddamnit! The Virginian who featured in the train of thought the half-breed endeavoured to keep out of his mind! Along with the kind of thinking that visualised himself putting down roots, the way Steele had!

But not as a horse breeder, running a three-thousand acre spread in some California valley: maybe a pillar of the local community now! All that took planning and patience: single-minded dedication to achieving an ambition to rebuild something approaching the kind of rich life fate had stolen from the man.

Edge was not a planner. He had little patience in that respect. And he did not possess single-minded ambition to achieve anything specific, be it a replacement for what had been lost or something entirely new.

But he was searching for something, some purpose to his life. That was what had to change! Without a predetermined aim, there was risk he would finish up in some two-street town like Ross. Turn into somebody like Joel Washington, liveryman. Or Ray Grogan, henpecked husband. Paul Calhern, saloon-keeper: no, he had tried that in a place called The Lucky Break in some Texas town long ago.

Much more likely, he would end up an older version of Eddie: local hardnose who drank for effect rather than pleasure while he waited for trouble to start, maybe would start some himself if the fancy took him when the liquor hit the wrong spot.

So, Edge found himself contemplating, should he finish riding this trail that had led him through the Cascades and into the Siskiyou Forest spread over the western slopes of the Klamath Mountains? With a purpose that had never been single-minded. Instead, the trip had been motivated by an irritating curiosity about what he might find if he crossed the California line and located the Providence River Valley. Where, he had heard, Adam Steele had set up in business on a horse ranch called Trail's End.

He did not consider himself a friend of the Virginian. Hell, their trails had crossed only three times. Troubled times, when circumstances had allied them on the same side. But they could just as easily have been enemies—as they had been during the War Between the States...

But this was not a matter of a man being curious about how things had turned out for an erstwhile partner. It was just that they were two of a kind, a matched pair in terms of their basic characters and the way they had been living their lives when their paths converged on those three occasions.

But Steele, so Edge had heard, was leading a very different, settled existence now. And because of the affinity the half-breed felt for the Virginian, it was natural that he should be curious to discover if the new life-style was successful or if the Trail's End venture had gone wrong. For if a man like Adam Steele could stop drifting and make something of himself, then sure as hell so could Edge.

'You gotta be out of your mind if you figure we'll go for that!' somebody snarled.

The angry tone of voice jerked Edge out of deep thought. And for part of a second he was sure he had spoken aloud and the rebuttal was directed at him. But before that second was complete he saw that Eddie in front of the bar and Calhern behind it were staring with surprise toward the table where the poker game had come to an abrupt pause. While Mitchell was half risen from his chair and the other three men were glaring at him with the same degree of scorn Eddie had shared among all the patrons of the Golden Eagle earlier.

'Markers ain't worth the paper they're scrawled on unless you got somethin' of worth to back 'em with!' a man who had not been the first to speak said, less stridently.

'And they sure as hell ain't worth nothin' from a passin'-through stranger we'll likely never see again!' This again from the man who had interrupted Edge's failed mental exercise.

'But you people have taken me for eight hundred bucks!' Mitchell complained as he lowered his rump back in his chair. 'And I figure I've got the beating of him with this hand!'

The five cards in which Vincent Mitchell had so much faith were face down in a fan on the table in front of him. The two men who were so adamant that IOUs were unacceptable had folded. The fourth man, seated directly across the table from Mitchell, held his five cards in a stack on the palm of a hand, ran the tips of the forefinger and thumb on his other hand back and forth along their sides as he said:

'You were kind of hard set about the four hands to a school

16

rule awhile back, Mr Mitchell. Well, Cecil here, Seymour and me, we have this rule about not allowing any markers in the pot. And we never play the game of poker unless we can afford to lose. Right, boys?'

He spoke in a quiet, even tone: but there was an undercurrent in his voice that warned its softness was not a sign of weakness.

'Right, Prentice,' Cecil agreed. 'When we know we're gettin' in deeper than we should, we back off outta the game.'

'That sure is right,' Seymour added earnestly. 'Why, I guess all of us have folded hands we figure could've won the pot for us. But we knew we didn't have enough of the foldin' green to find out, one way or the other.'

'You don't have to tell me how a hand of poker's played!' Mitchell snapped.

'I'm sure we don't,' Prentice countered in the same mild-mannered way as before. 'Nor do I need to remind you, I'm certain, that it will cost you the amount of one hundred dollars to have me show, Mr Mitchell? Or you fold and I take the pot?'

The dudishly-garbed gambler abruptly looked haggard rather than dissipated. He licked his lips rapidly and mopped absently at his pale face with a handkerchief: the sweat not oozing from his pores because of the temperature of the spring evening. For the recently ended winter was still discernible in the Oregon air once the sun dipped into the not too distant Pacific Ocean. Then he began to knead the handkerchief between his sticky palms, stared fixedly at the heap of bills and dollar coins on the centre of the table.

'Well, are you going to fold, Mr Mitchell?' Prentice asked, not quite as mildly as before, an undercurrent of impatience in his tone.

'Or you gonna ante up the hundred bucks?' Cecil urged eagerly.

'In cash or in kind, mister?' Seymour reminded. And in his voice, the look on his face and the way he leaned forward there was undisguised avariciousness.

This caused Edge to suspect all three local men were in line for a share of the pot if Mitchell could not call, or he could but

17

his hand was no match for Prentice's cards. Which was none of his business, the half-breed told himself as he finished the heeltaps of beer in his glass.

While Prentice, Cecil and Seymour were urging Mitchell to take some form of action, the man at the centre of attention dragged his agitated gaze away from the money to look at each of his fellow players in turn, then at Edge, Calhern and Eddie: finally down at the fan of five cards on the table.

'No good lookin' at me, mister,' Eddie growled in his studiedly tough voice as he toyed with his carefully-shaped moustache. 'Gamblin' ain't a vice of mine. So ... Hey, I can't give you no ad*vice*!'

He considered the clumsy play on words was uproariously funny and vented a loud belly laugh. But curtailed the sound after he looked around and saw nobody else shared his good humour.

Then he scowled as he turned to face across the bar counter again, complained to the saloonkeeper: 'Guess nobody got it, uh?' He threw back the whiskey in one, banged his glass down, groaned: 'This sure is some kinda fun place you run here, Calhern!'

'I run a saloon, Eddie,' Calhern answered dully. 'I sell booze. What my customers do while they're drinkin' it is none of my concern. Long as they don't cause trouble.'

He did not shift his attention away from the source of potential trouble: the table where four men still sat, one of them glaring angrily at the other three who waited with mounting impatience for a response to the ultimatum they had issued.

Mitchell was experiencing a greater degree of frustration now, and Edge wondered if the man had come to the same conclusion he had: that the pot was to be shared, which meant the game had been loaded three to one from the start.

Edge again told himself it was none of his business. Then he asked himself if he needed a shot or two of liquor to help the beer kill the aftertaste of the food.

Eddie banged his shot glass on the bartop. Giggled a signal that he had started to feel the liquor and beer mix hitting the right spot. Then he slurred: 'Well, give me another drink and let

18

the other folks wallow in their misery while I have a little fun, Calhern.'

He giggled again, took a swig of beer, belched and swung around to survey the saloon, a lopsided grin on his face. After he failed to capture the attention of any of the card players, who suddenly all leaned forward to put their heads together, deep in secret discussion, he fixed his glassy gaze on Edge, asked sneeringly:

'How about you, stranger?'

'How about me? Edge countered.

'Ain't you got a sense of humour? Don't you enjoy a joke?'

'Sure,' Edge told him evenly, shifted his eyes away from the drunk to look to where Mitchell suddenly rose from the table with a grunt of qualified satisfaction as the other three card players looked up at him with a mixture of incredulity and eager anticipation. 'But there are some jokers who just ain't funny.'

'Do me a favour, mister?' Mitchell asked of Edge.

Eddie did not understand exactly what had been said to him, but was convinced he had been insulted. He demanded to know: 'You lookin' to make trouble, stranger?'

Edge returned his gaze to the drunk, put more ice into the glinting slits of his eyes as he answered: 'No, feller. What I'm looking for is private. What I see of you, you're just a part of that.'

'Uh?' Eddie was totally perplexed.

'What did you ever do for me?' Edge asked of Mitchell.

Calhern vented a genuine belly laugh, said when it ended: 'It's a funnier joke than the one you made, Eddie!'

Which intrigued Edge for a moment. Until he realised that Calhern knew when one of his regular customers had downed enough liquor to be used as the butt of humour without taking violent offence.

'It's not like that, mister,' Mitchell said. 'Won't cost you anything except a little time. And it'll be worth ten bucks out of the pot if I win it.'

'What if you don't?'

Mitchell managed to check the threat of a flare of anger by

venting a sigh. He sounded strained when he insisted: 'You'll only be putting up some time. I'm not asking you to risk anything.'

With each moment that passed he was having greater difficulty holding on to his temper: the typical gambler convinced he is on to a sure thing and cannot understand how others don't have the faith to back his judgment.

'How much time are we talking about?'

'Long as it takes me to get to the Grogan boarding house and back here. I'd say no more than five minutes tops?'

'So time really is money,' Edge said. 'What are you buying at two bucks a minute?'

'Your attention.' He shrugged. 'And your neutrality, I guess.'

'Get to the point!' Cecil urged.

'Like for you to keep a careful eye on this hand of mine.' Mitchell waved at the fan of cards on the table in front of his recently vacated chair. 'Ensure nobody fools with it until I return?'

'Sir, you can rely upon Cecil, Seymour and myself not to interfere with——'

'I'm a gambler!' Mitchell cut in on the indignant Prentice. 'But I do not like to take unnecessary chances when I gamble with strangers. No offence intended, and as gambling men yourselves, I'm sure you gentlemen will take my point. I alone know the value of my cards and I need an independent witness to see that their value remains the same while I am absent.'

'What d'you mean, no damn offence?' Seymour snapped.

'Easy now,' Prentice placated, and spread his cards in a fan on the table in front of him. 'It'll be in our interest as well. If—although I feel it is more like *when*—my hand beats that of Mr Mitchell, he will not be able to claim he was cheated.'

'That's right,' Mitchell agreed eagerly. 'A third party with no financial interest in the game, except the token fee I have offered, will ensure there has been no fooling with either hand.'

Seymour and Cecil both looked about to press the point about being offended. But Prentice spoke first, allowed with a nod:

'Very well, Mr Mitchell. I am prepared to go along with this.' He looked over at Edge, smiled as he promised: 'And in the event I win the pot, I will pay the fee of ten dollars for the services of the independent third party?'

'The money's as neutral as I am,' Edge said as he rose from his table. 'It doesn't matter to me who pays me.'

After a final glance at his cards in the fan on the table in the opposite corner of the saloon, Mitchell hurried out of the Golden Eagle without looking back.

Eddie picked up his latest whiskey, knocked it back in one and slurred scornfully: 'What's with this third party shit? We ain't even had a first party yet! With the bunch of deadbeats you got in here tonight, Calhern! Hey, what the ...'

He was startled by the sound of Edge's tread close behind him. And he whirled, his moustache no longer making him look hard now his deep-set eyes were filled with fear while he worried he had said something that stirred rage within the tall, lean, impassive-faced, gun-toting stranger.

But Edge merely glanced coldly at him without pausing as he went past, toward the table where there was now an empty chair, the footfalls of its previous occupant still audible but diminishing fast along the street outside.

'Yeah, feller,' the half-breed directed over his shoulder as Eddie did not quite manage to hold in another belch. 'I'm a real party pooper.' Then he swept his glinting-eyed gaze over the trio of men still seated around the table, added: 'Hired on to see there's no fooling around with a game.'

2

Edge ignored the vacated chair and leaned his back against the wall nearby. Looked at the two hands of cards rather than the three men avidly interested in which would win the heap of money, but took the time to revise his opinion about them.

Close up, he saw they were not as elderly as he had thought at first impression: allowed he had probably made this inconsequential mistake because he had not been in the frame of mind to look at anything or anybody closely since he rode into this lumber town and at once began to think of it in terms of being one of the last places in the world where he would wish to finish up, end his drifting existence and put down roots.

'Prentice Harper, sir.'

The man with a poker hand he thought could beat that of Vincent Mitchell introduced himself to Edge with the kind of smile that can sometimes be detected on the faces of predatory animals in skilfully-executed paintings. Close to sixty, he was growing old gracefully: his grey hair neatly cut and slicked down, his leanly handsome face newly shaved for the evening visit to the saloon, his blue eyes clear and bright, his fingernails clean and trimmed.

His outfit, the check shirt and denim pants of a working man, was far from new but it was clean and crisply cared for, like he had not undertaken any manual labour in the clothes for a long time. Maybe never. He smelled of a little too much pomade and talcum powder.

The half full glass of beer which stood between his hand of cards and his diminished pile of stake money was flat.

'I'm Seymour Singer,' the man on Harper's right said without enthusiasm, but showed a brief broad smile with

22

yellow dentures too large for his mouth.

He was closer to Edge's age than to Harper's. Taller and thinner than Harper by a head and fifty pounds, his face almost skeletal, with deep set eyes that were piercingly bright: dark in the dimly lamplit saloon. He was also freshly shaved, but was not clean shaven. Wore a strange set of whiskers which consisted of an inch-wide moustache that spanned the flare of his nostrils and a small pointed beard that sprouted from the centre of his jaw. The whiskers looked to be dyed black, contrasting vividly with his fine head of hair that was brownish blond.

He wore a cream-coloured suit that was store-bought, probably supplied by a country tailor: for although it was almost brand new, the style was old-fashioned, like the design had been copied from an out-of-date mail order catalogue. Or maybe Seymour Singer just had quaint tastes in clothes.

'Cecil Wyler,' the third member of the trio greeted, his smile more spontaneous and so perhaps more genuine than the others. 'And you are...?'

'Edge.' He tipped his hat to all three of them.

'As in sharp or jagged or teeth on or——'

'Over the,' he interrupted the still-grinning Wyler. 'Hope you fellers won't try to put anything over on me?'

The short and fat, round-faced man decided to abandon for the moment his role as the comedian of the group: could not sustain his cheerful manner in face of the cold gaze from the half-breed's narrowed, hooded eyes. He had not shaved for the evening on the town, had a day's growth of black bristles that emphasised the shiny paleness of his bald skull in a horseshoe of grey hair. He was about the same age as Singer and also like Singer he had an empty shot glass alongside his small pile of stake money.

His rotund frame was clothed in pants that were too tight, a matching vest that was frayed and had two buttons missing, a grubby white shirt and an askew bow tie.

Edge thought that individually the men might appear to be harmless store clerks or office penpushers: maybe faithful husbands and doting fathers. But as a group, waiting with

23

barely-controlled impatience for something extraordinary to happen, they emanated a strange kind of menace that warned they should not be taken for granted: they were much more dangerous than they might appear at first impression.

'There's no fear of that, Mr Edge,' Harper answered. He was plainly the dominant member of the group in every situation—not just when he held a hand of poker they were all convinced would win a rich pot plus whatever mysterious bonus Mitchell had gone to bring. 'I'm sure we can all appreciate Mr Mitchell's concern. He's a stranger to town, engaged in a card game with three good friends. There isn't one of us at this table who would not take steps to protect his interests in some way were any of us in a similar situation.'

Edge thought Harper was using empty talk as a release for tension: maybe to keep himself from worrying that his cards might after all not be better than those of the absent man.

But Cecil Wyler had no such doubts, said: 'Especially when there's so much at stake!'

He licked his lips, as Mitchell had earlier. But whereas Mitchell had been nervously anxious, Wyler was pleasurably eager.

'Shit, that don't look like so much to me!' Eddie sneered from the bar. He waved his glass and spilled some of its contents. 'Even if there was another hundred in it, there wouldn't be much more than a grand in the pot, looks like! Why, up in Portland once, I saw a——'

'Money isn't everything, Mr Noon,' Harper interrupted, even toned, but with an irritated glint in his eyes.

'Uh?' Noon growled. He was drunkenly perplexed again, poised to be more contemptuous than ever.

'It's not what makes the world go round,' Wyler said cryptically, smiling again.

Singer laughed at the secret joke.

'What the hell, why all the——' Noon started.

'It's love does that, isn't that what they say?' Wyler asked rhetorically. 'And if Mitchell is as good as his word, Prentice's hand is as good as he thinks it is, well——'

'Let's just wait and see, shall we?' Harper cut in, and tilted his

24

head to one side in a listening attitude.

Only Noon failed to see this and he made to demand an explanation. But he was signalled into silence by Calhern, who then used one of his big, soft hands to indicate the batwinged doorway of the saloon. Where everybody except for Edge was looking, all of them now hearing the approaching footfalls that had first captured Harper's attention.

The three men at the corner table were clearly listening intently for something other than the mere footfalls that marked the return to the Golden Eagle of Vincent Mitchell.

'It sounds to me like he don't have——' Singer started.

'I said to wait and see!' Harper rasped.

Edge looked sharply at him, for a moment glimpsed an expression that matched the harshness of his tone. Before Harper realised that he had revealed a side of himself he would have preferred to keep concealed in the present circumstances and quickly replaced the scowl with a smile, moderated his voice to add:

'All will be revealed very soon now.'

'We surely hope so!' Wyler blurted. 'If it's as good as he claimed!'

He laughed, but cut it off short as all ears were cocked to listen with greater concentration than ever as the sound of the man's approach became more pronounced, his footfalls rapping on a sidewalk now. And now, too, there were other sounds. Of other footfalls, much lighter in tread. And quicker, like those of a child who needed to almost run to keep up with a long legged, more heavily built man.

There was no sidewalk immediately out front of the Golden Eagle, and just the man's footsteps were audible again on the hard-packed dirt of the street for a final few seconds. Then he halted and in the sudden silence all the eyes that were turned toward the doorway did not even blink.

The half-breed continued to look down at the two fans of cards at either side of the heap of money in the pot, but he could see the saloon entrance on the periphery of his vision.

A hand was hooked over the top of a batwing, pushed it part way open. It could have been any man's hand, but it was definitely Vincent Mitchell's not quite cultured voice which instructed:

'All right, woman. In you go.'

Paul Calhern exclaimed: 'Hot damn!'

'Holy shit!' Eddie Noon rasped.

Cecil Wyler and Seymour Singer just stared, seemingly dumbstruck with their mouths hanging open.

The only sign of emotion Prentice Harper showed was a moistening rather than a licking of his lips: his tongue twice darting out and recoiling fast, as if he were tasting the atmosphere. Like a lizard or snake sensing prey nearby.

Edge's reaction was even less pronounced than this: a pursing of his thin lips.

'Gentlemen, this is Ruby Red,' Mitchell announced as he moved to stand alongside the half-breed he had ushered on to the threshold of the Golden Eagle. There was just a slight tremor in his tone.

'Hot damn,' Calhern muttered again.

Mitchell went on: 'My collateral for the hundred dollar ante I must make for Mr Harper to show.'

'Holy shit!' Noon repeated, but far less loudly than before. And he seemed suddenly to have sobered up as he turned fully around, leaned his back against the bar counter, to get himself a better view of the half white woman-half squaw across the dimly lamplit room.

Mitchell clearly enjoyed the effect triggered by the appearance of Ruby Red: smiled in satisfaction that it was at least as good as he had expected. Celebrated by angling a fat cigar from a side of his mouth, lighting it with a match struck on the door jamb.

The woman herself appeared totally unmoved by the startled attention focused upon her. She was not aloof, nor afraid, nor proud nor disgusted: did not respond in any way that a normal woman would in this situation, in Edge's estimation.

Hell, she stood there like a prize animal! Displayed for sale before the arrogantly appraising gazes of potential purchasers. A fine-looking animal with the intelligence either to be supremely confident of its attractions, or simply knows from past experience it cannot do anything to prevent what is happening: so is dolefully resigned to whatever fate awaits.

Ruby Red certainly had attractions for the men who eyed her in the Golden Eagle Saloon this evening. She was about twenty five, just a couple of inches under six feet tall and maybe a little underweight for that height. But although she was slender, she was definitely a well developed woman: this seen in the ample thrusts of her breasts temptingly contoured by the homespun fabric of a loose-fitting red shirt, and the prominent swell of her hips under a floral-patterned skirt held snug around her narrow waist by a broad belt. The skirt reached almost to her bare ankles above feet shod in moccasins.

So she was no small child and it was the close fit of the skirt around her long legs that had meant she needed to half run to keep pace with Mitchell out on the street.

Jammed on her head, as if in haste, was a low-crowned, floppy wide-brimmed hat from beneath which spilled long blonde hair that fell below her shoulders, dull and tangled from lack of brushing right then.

The hat and hair and buttoned-up shirt framed a face that was not beautiful, not lovely, nor pretty. No such conventional terms could be applied to this woman's features. For her cheekbones were just a little too low, the nose a little too broad, the eyes too far apart, the mouth too wide and her chin too pointed to be conventionally attractive.

But neither was she in any way homely. Instead, the less than perfect features formed into a combination that exuded a brooding sexuality which was far more appealing to a man than mere skin-deep beauty.

Anyway, that was how Edge felt when he found his gaze held by that of the dark-coloured eyes of Ruby Red: thought she looked at him for just a fraction of a second longer than at any of the other men. But he was prepared to allow that maybe this was only in his imagination, a wishful thought. Likewise the notion that her coldly impassive expression was relieved by a glimmer of warmth in that fleeting moment while their eyes met. When perhaps she recognised from something in his face that he was seeing her as a whole person. Albeit a woman he admired for her sexuality, but not solely as an object of lust.

None of which mattered, he acknowledged the next moment. For she was obviously a whore, or something very close to it, to submit without protest to such a degrading experience.

Then Vincent Mitchell stepped from between the batwings, which flapped close behind him as he removed the cigar from his mouth, said: 'She has agreed to do what is required of her, Mr Harper. To wit, should I lose the hand, Ruby Red will consent to go with you willingly. And I think you have to agree, sight largely unseen as it were, one hundred dollars is something of an under-valuation of what such a fine woman has to offer a man?'

'When all is revealed, I bet that sure is right!' Wyler murmured in breathless admiration, explaining his cryptic remark of a minute ago.

Singer swallowed hard, asked huskily: 'She understands what's meant by goin' with Prentice? Not just for a——'

'Damnit, no!' Calhern protested, his small eyes shining with anger as saliva sprayed from between his fleshy lips.

'What'd he say?' Singer growled, unable to tear his gaze away from the woman as he got ready to be just as mad as the saloonkeeper if Calhern did anything to prevent the wager taking place.

'What is your objection, Calhern?' Harper asked. 'The young lady is quite clearly a willing participant?'

Calhern dragged his bug-eyed gaze away from Ruby Red, wiped the back of a hand across his mouth, said huskily: 'You gents ain't been in town too long. But you saw my wife before she left. Peg ain't never allowed no loose women in our place. She ain't that kind. And just because she's away in Medford visitin' her——'

'Mr Calhern, Ruby Red is no whore!' Mitchell broke in indignantly.

He curled an arm around the woman's shoulders while she continued to gaze directly ahead, did not respond to what he said nor to his touch as he went on:

'She is I suppose what one could term my common law wife. And, like any good wife, she has agreed to obey the wishes of her husband.'

'And if we happen to——' Wyler started excitedly.

Harper cleared his throat noisily to call attention to the man's slip of the tongue over the pronoun, glared at him.

'If *Prentice* should happen to win the game, Calhern,' the short fat man went on, almost slavering as he ran his gaze up and down the woman who stood so sensually submissively on the threshold, 'it won't be in the Golden Eagle that——'

Eddie Noon cut in on the eager Wyler: 'Shit, if I was you guys, I wouldn't go along with the bet!'

There was a brand of viciousness in his tone that captured all attention. Even the woman looked at him with a flash of hatred in her eyes that burned into his face like she could read what he was about to say from his tone. Thought she could force the words back down his throat with the intense power of her stare.

'She's just a Goddamn half-breed,' the scowling Noon went on, thumbs hooked over the ornate buckle of his belt. 'That ain't worth no hundred bucks, seems to me. Fifty tops, I figure. For the white in her.'

Having caught his drift, the fire went out of Ruby Red before he was through and she reverted to her unblinking gaze into the middle distance.

Which surprised nobody. While all of them might have been intrigued to see that Edge did react to the sneered insult: narrowed his eyes to the merest slivers of glinting ice blue as his body stiffened.

'Quit that kinda talk, Noon!' Calhern snapped. 'I'll have no bigotry in my place. Same as I won't have immorality. I still can't be sure if I oughta allow this kind of crazy gamblin' in the Golden Eagle. It sticks in my craw, a man bettin' a woman on a hand of cards. And I'm damn sure Peg wouldn't——'

'So why don't we go out on the street and finish the damn game, Prentice?' Singer growled and made to rise from his chair.

But he sat down hard again as Edge reached across him and he thought the half-breed was intent on preventing him from doing what he wanted. Then the man with the oversize false teeth expressed sheepishness in the wake of fear when the half-breed asked evenly:

'Pardon me, feller.'

29

He reached into the money in the pot on the centre of the table and extracted two five dollar bills. Which he then held up, displaying the money first to Harper and then Mitchell, said: 'My fee, okay?'

'Okay,' Calhern echoed as the two men directly involved in the poker showdown curtly nodded their agreement to what Edge had done and said.

Then the uneasy saloonkeeper amplified his assent that the game could be played to its end on his premises. 'Just finish up and then get the hell out of here.'

From the way he started to sweat, the thickness of his voice and the light in his constantly blinking eyes, it was plain that Calhern was getting a sexual thrill out of witnessing the betting of a woman's favours against the showing of a poker hand.

'I appreciate that, Mr Calhern,' Harper said, and now his voice was a little husky as he beckoned for Mitchell to approach the table.

'Me, too,' Mitchell said, replaced the cigar between his teeth and steered Ruby Red toward the table. He spoke around the cigar then. 'It won't take long. And as I've maintained from the outset, I'm confident I will carry the day, and so the question of immorality is academic. Wait there, my dear.'

Edge pushed the ten dollars into a hip pocket and moved away from the wall.

Mitchell nodded to him and resumed his seat, waving that the woman should stand beside his chair. Then he looked long and hard at the fan of cards on the table before him, like he had memorised the precise position of each of them, was satisfying himself they had not been moved by a fraction of an inch.

Not until Edge had moved far enough away from the table so he could not glimpse the faces of the cards did Mitchell pick them up. He closed them into a stack, then opened them out into another, narrower fan in both hands. And a mixture of relief and pleasure melded on his features before he nodded to the man across the table from him, motioned with his head toward the woman, stated his bet:

'Ruby Red to see what you hold, Mr Harper.'

They were all full-blooded male animals of the human

species who waited and watched to learn the fate of the lone female of their kind. None was immune to the atmosphere of blatant lust with an undercurrent of violence that existed within the quiet, dimly-lit saloon. Even Mitchell, who was totally confident the woman would remain his property, found her familiar face and form arousing in this highly charged situation.

But he did not look at her after he made the bet, though. Chose not to watch her standing as statue-like as ever while men directed their lascivious gazes at her and drew not the slightest reaction from her: by word, expression or even a tremor within her tall, lean, lithe body.

Then, one at a time, Harper lifted and turned over the cards of his hand. And the attention of the men not directly engaged in the showdown began to switch constantly between the tabletop and the woman.

While Harper shifted his gaze back and forth between the woman and Mitchell, for he had memorised the order and value of the cards in his hand, named them correctly in sequence as he turned them face up, without need to see them.

'Ace of Hearts... Ace of Diamonds... Ace of Clubs.'

When he started, his face had been empty of expression. But then he showed the quietest of smiles as he watched the woman exclusively, raking his gaze from the top of her hatted head to her moccasinned feet. And all the while his tongue darted out and back again, the look in his eyes suggesting that he could actually taste the flavour of her flesh rather than just the air now.

Edge thought that at last Ruby Red was reacting to the tension of her situation: had begun to breathe a little faster, a little more deeply. Or maybe, he allowed, this was in his imagination again. As he found his glittering-eyed gaze fixed upon the rise and fall of her breasts within the shirt. It could be her breathing and the way it moved her upper body had always been this pronounced.

Vincent Mitchell began to smile around the cigar as one, then another and a third ace was lifted, turned over and named. He remained certain he had the winning hand as he estimated the value of Harper's still unseen cards. Became increasingly convinced the other man's hand was not strong enough to win the pot and the compliant body of Ruby Red. And finally he could not contain his gambler's excitement any longer, blurted:

'Even if you got two kings, sir, your top full house will not beat——'

'Ace of Spades,' Harper broke in, and the smile of pleasurable anticipation he had been directing at the woman became a leer which did not alter as he turned his head to look across the table at Mitchell. Then, by a just discernible twist of his mouthline and a narrowing of his blue eyes he showed an expression that conveyed almost childish glee at winning for winning's sake, no matter what the prize.

This while Mitchell's face underwent a radical change of shape: from excitement to devastation as the cigar dropped out of his fallen open mouth, bounced off the table and hit the floor in a shower of glowing tobacco embers.

'... my four tens,' he completed in a lame, barely audible voice.

'Son-of-one-hell-of-a-friggin'-bitch!' Noon muttered hoarsely.

'All of us make mistakes,' Harper said to Mitchell. 'There aren't too many hands can beat what you have, but——'

'You don't have to tell me about poker!' Mitchell rasped in a voice that sounded like a hand was clutched around his throat.

Once they had seen Harper turn over a seven of hearts and Mitchell let his cards fall face up to reveal he had a jack with his four tens, everyone else had returned their eyes to the woman.

Perhaps some of them saw, like Edge, a slight smile of triumph cross her face in the blinking of an eye. But Mitchell did not see this smile that was directed at him, discreetly releasing her feelings at the way his over-confidence had been destroyed by the turning over of that final ace. Like Ruby Red had seen him only ever triumph in similar situations, none of which had ever resulted in anything good for her.

Or maybe she had always hated his guts in every situation: simply got pleasure from seeing him cut down to size, humiliated as he had humiliated her. Or maybe she relished the prospect of leaving him, no matter what was in store for her with Harper and his two partners. Maybe...

Or maybe it was none of his business, Edge rebuked himself, swung away from the table and went toward the bar as he delved a hand into a shirt pocket for the makings. Ruby Red was nothing to him, so he had no reason to be concerned with why she did anything: be it smiling a secret smile at a man's mortification or condoning the humiliating indignity of allowing herself to pass from one man to another as a bet in a poker game.

'Hell of a thing, uh?' Calhern asked Edge, and ran a hand across his saliva-wet mouth again. Then jutted out his lower lip to blow a cooling stream of air up over his sweat-beaded face. Struggling to overcome his sexual arousal.

'Yeah,' the half-breed agreed. 'I'll take a shot of rye, feller?'

'Sure thing.' Calhern took down a bottle off a shelf, reached a glass out from under the bar counter and put them both on top.

'Reckon I'll have another,' Noon said as Calhern uncorked the bottle. He pulled a face, shook his head, complained: 'Suddenly it don't feel like I've hardly had a drink yet tonight.'

'You've had three bucksworth, which includes this one, Eddie,' the saloonkeeper told him as he first filled Edge's fresh glass, then the frequently used one of the younger man.

There was some low-toned talk at the table where Harper was gathering in the money from the pot and Singer and Wyler put away what was left of their stakes. While the woman continued to stand with her feet together, her arms at her sides, head held to peer straight in front of her. And Mitchell sat slumped in his chair, hands cupped at either side of the five cards that had lost him money and Ruby Red.

'I ain't gonna give you no argument on what I owe,' Noon growled. He threw back the whiskey in one, banged the glass down for a refill. 'Just so you realise I ain't really gettin' no more liquored-up than usual on a Saturday night, okay?'

Calhern shrugged his wide shoulders, answered evenly: 'Sellin' liquor is my business, like I told you awhile back. And I'll keep sellin' it to anyone so long as they don't make trouble in my place.'

He started out looking between Noon and Edge, but when

he made mention of trouble his attention was once again drawn to the table where trouble had simmered ever since Mitchell made his then secret deal with the other three men.

And now trouble came a long step closer.

'No, it's just not possible!'

Mitchell's protest was violently accompanied by the crash of his chair tipping over backwards with the force of the abrupt rise to his feet.

'Oh, no,' Calhern groaned, his fleshy face more doleful looking than ever.

Noon whirled.

Edge, in process of rolling a cigarette, turned more slowly to look toward the four men and one woman at the table, cleared now of money, but still littered with cards. They were locked in a frozen tableau for a stretched second, all of them as unmoving as Ruby Red had been while she awaited her fate which depended on the whims of a poker game.

Then she was the first to move, backed away a pace and turned her head to peer at Edge. And now there was definitely a look in her dark eyes especially for him—a pleading for him to help.

Beyond her, Vincent Mitchell stood erect, right hand inside his suit jacket, under the left lapel. Cecil Wyler was also up on his feet, but his flabby body was awkwardly curved in an attitude that looked uncomfortable. But he held it from fear of what it was that Mitchell was going to jerk out from under his suit jacket. The two men who remained seated expressed a lesser degree of trepidation.

'I think...' Harper started.

'I've been cheated!' Mitchell snarled, and sprang his right hand into sight, fisted around the butt of a .31 calibre Remington-Rider revolver. A small gun with a three-inch barrel that weighed less than threequarters of a pound complete with its five shells. From the way Mitchell backed off, increasing the range but giving himself a better field of fire over the entire saloon, the Remington was fully loaded and he was confident he could hit whoever he fired at if circumstances made it necessary to use the small gun.

Ruby Red spoke for the first time in a voice that did not betray a trace of any accent that came from the Indian side of her heritage: 'Vinny, don't be such a——'

'Shut up, woman!' he barked. 'Just do what I tell you. Like always.'

· 'You're making an even bigger mistake this time, Mitchell,' Harper warned, quickly recovered from surprise. He signalled with a wave of his hand for Wyler to sit down.

'Don't think he won't carry through any threat he makes,' Ruby Red warned grimly.

'Damn right!' Mitchell confirmed. 'I'll kill any man who tries to stop me getting back what was stolen from me.'

'Nobody stole anything from——' Singer made to protest.

'There had to be some cheating!' Mitchell broke in. Like before, with Ruby Red and Prentice Harper, he swung his angry gaze and the muzzle of the gun toward the speaker. 'My hand was just like I left it. But I figure Harper switched his while I was gone to bring Ruby——'

'No, mister, that ain't necessary!'

It was Paul Calhern who blurted this and captured all attention. But just for a moment, before all eyes focused on Edge. Who had finished rolling his cigarette, hung it at the side of his mouth, turned to face Mitchell: his hand dropped down from his face to hover, slightly curved, close to his holstered Colt.

Ruby Red vented a gasp of shock and took another backward step. Made sure she was clear of the line of fire between Mitchell and Edge.

Mitchell was unable to move a muscle after he turned his head to see Edge, saw the look on the half-breed's face, heard the tone of his voice when he warned:

'You swing that gun to aim it at me, I'll kill you. On account of I don't like to have guns aimed at me. Especially it irritates me after I've given the warning.'

'Mister, please don't involve yourself in——' Ruby Red attempted to implore.

'I'm not through yet, lady,' Edge told her without shifting his unblinking gaze away from Mitchell. 'You also have to know,

I'll kill you if you don't take back what you just said about me cheating you, feller.'

Mitchell swallowed hard, croaked: 'I never accused you! I said it to Harper. I guess he was able to do it without you——'

A gunshot rang out. And Edge slapped his hand instinctively to the jutting butt of the Frontier Colt. Fisted it tight, then froze with the revolver only halfway out of the holster as he saw the blood on Mitchell's face, spilling down from a hole in the centre of his forehead.

Then he saw the shot had been fired by a gun in the fist of Prentice Harper, the heel of the man's hand wrapped around the butt of the derringer resting on the tabletop, barrel angled up to draw a bead on the head of the man standing across from him.

A moment later Mitchell was not standing there. He died on his feet and staggered backwards, gun hand dropping to his side, revolver slipping from his lifeless grip as he tripped on his overturned chair and collapsed into an ungainly heap, belly arched obscenely upwards, across it.

'Holy shit!' Eddie Noon exclaimed for the third time.

'Oh my God, there's been a killin' in the Golden Eagle,' Calhern gasped.

Edge said evenly: 'You want to give me a good reason why I shouldn't kill *you*?'

All gazes swivelled fast toward him, like nobody could be sure who it was he addressed the question to. And they found him looking at Harper, who now had no gun in either of the hands he splayed on the tabletop. It had been spirited away as deftly as it had been conjured up, seemingly out of nowhere, a few seconds earlier.

Harper darted his tongue out and back in, inclined his head, answered in a conversational tone with just a slight sign of strain on his handsome face: 'Item, Mr Edge, I'm not aiming a weapon at you. Item, although I understand your point of view, it was I Mitchell accused of being a cheat. By implication, he considered you no more than a conspirator. Item, I therefore considered it was my honour that was called into more serious question.'

36

Behind his impassive outer shell Edge felt rage still burning almost painfully inside him as he listened to the soft-spoken words of Prentice Harper. He also had the impression of eyes boring into him with palpable force as everyone waited fearfully for his response.

Then he was able to control the emotion, confine it into an ice cold ball at the pit of his stomach: and thus the urge to kill a man who had used him as a distraction so that he could kill another was suddenly gone. But he still harboured a compelling need to unleash his frustration against something or somebody.

Which did not show as he thrust the Colt all the way back into the holster: an action that drew audible sighs of relief from Calhern, Wyler and Ruby Red. While Singer continued to show unease and Harper expressed a just discernible smile.

'And all of this because of some lousy half-breed!' Eddie Noon said, giggled, banged his empty glass down on the counter top to reveal this first drink after the end of the tense game and then the shooting had made him drunk again. 'I'll have another, bartender!'

'Nobody gets any more drinks until I've got the corpse out of my place!' Calhern snarled.

Edge figured enough cooling down time had elapsed for him to be sure he was going to do the right thing to relieve his feelings without causing some damage that might land him in serious trouble in this town.

He turned slowly toward Eddie Noon, was in process of altering his grin into a scowl at what Calhern had said. Then he speeded the turn into a whirl, brought up his right hand fisted more tightly than it had been around the butt of the revolver. Slammed it into Noon's jaw with enough force to power the drunk up off his feet, on to the bar, slither him along it and off the far end: where he crashed to the floor with his own and Edge's glass shattered beneath him.

After a stretched second of silence, Calhern asked in an incredulous tone: 'Why'd you do that to him, mister?'

'I'm as much of a half-breed as the lady, feller,' Edge replied around the cigarette still angled from the side of his mouth. 'He sounded off about the kind of people we are and I didn't like it. I'll cover the cost of the damage. Plus what I owe for the food and drink.'

Calhern vented a sound that was like a laugh that he tried to control because the circumstances made good humour inappropriate. Then he shook his head, told Edge resolutely: 'Oh no you won't, mister.'

'I always pay my way,' Edge replied flatly, and drew one of the newly-earned five spots out of his pocket, placed it on the bartop.

Calhern looked like he was about to argue the point, then shrugged, made change from a pocket in the front of his apron, said: 'Okay, if that's the way you want it. But only for the chow and the beer and the shot of liquor, mister.'

He directed a look of malevolent enjoyment toward the unconscious man at the far end of the counter. 'I've waited a long time to see that tough-talkin' bastard cut down to his right size. About the only thing I've got a laugh out of tonight. Seein' Noon take off and zoom along the counter and——'

'Yeah, feller, it's what happens when you're having fun,' Edge broke in.

'Uh?'

The half-breed made a sideways motion with his hand above the counter as he turned away from it, replied: 'Time flies.'

3

A burst of low-toned talk sounded against the flapping of the batwing doors after Edge left the Golden Eagle. But he made no attempt to hear what was said as, for a few moments, he nurtured his final impression of the interior of the saloon: a look in the dark eyes of Ruby Red which he got only occasionally from a woman, and mostly not from the kind he found attractive.

The majority of women considered his leanly-constructed Aryan-Latin facial mix disturbing, even repulsive. But every once in awhile a woman would eye him as did Ruby Red as he went out of the Golden Eagle—with undisguised admiration, unashamed to be intrigued about the kind of complicated man who lay behind the far from classically handsome, always faintly menacing exterior. And sometimes he felt himself drawn to such a woman, like tonight with...

But he had already resolved not to play any further part in the life of this half-breed woman! And he firmed this decision as he moved through the chill, brightly moonlit night, ambling north along the quiet main street of Ross, toward the intersection with the town's only other street at the far end. He was going to have himself a sound night's sleep in the Grogan boarding house on the south west corner of the intersection, undisturbed by foolish notions bred by the whims of a vivid imagination, and ride out of town at dawn.

Not for the first time, though, he discovered that roads to a lot of places other than hell can be paved with good intentions.

He managed to get a good and solid six hours of sleep despite a body of muffled sound that started up soon after he bedded down in a second floor room at the rear of the boarding house. For there

39

was nothing remotely clamorous about the noise as news of the killing at the Golden Eagle circulated and the more curious of Ross's citizens converged on the saloon in search of the details.

At least, this was the reason Edge figured out as the cause of the unobtrusive sounds—footfalls, voices, hooves and the wheels of a wagon on a hard-packed street surface—as he lay in the comfortable, fresh-smelling bed: prepared to fill his mind with any kind of inconsequential thoughts if they kept out erotic notions and images which featured Ruby Red.

His next conscious act was to snap open his eyes to the first light of a new day. And at the same moment he smelled coffee and ham and eggs about ready to become somebody's breakfast: these aromas working to undermine his decision to make a start out of this town at crack of dawn.

He did not pussyfoot on the stairway, nor make any token protest when the forty-years-old, overweight and garishly-blonde haired Maud Grogan called out for him to come into the kitchen. Where her husband already sat at a scrubbed pine table and gave Edge a nod and a smile before he started in on the food placed before him.

While the woman fixed a similar meal of ham and eggs and grits which she reminded the half-breed he had paid for in advance as part of his room rent yesterday, he had himself a hot water shave in the kitchen.

This luxury would not cost him anything extra, Maud Grogan assured him. Even though it was so hard for her to make ends meet running a boarding house like this in a town like Ross that Ray had to take a job outside of the business, working as a teamster for the McAllister Lumber Company. Still she endeavoured to make her roomers feel as comfortable as possible without overcharging them.

Her stockily-built, bald-headed and bright-eyed husband, older by ten years, was required only to contribute an occasional affirmative or negative response to rhetorical questions while he sat at the table finishing his breakfast. And Edge needed only to listen as he shaved.

Then Ray, washed and shaved and fully dressed already, brushed his lips across his wife's cheek and gave Edge a compassionate look along with a cheerful goodbye before he left the kitchen and went out of the house.

Edge had finished shaving by then, and Maud Grogan ushered him into the chair across the table from where Ray had sat. A minute or so later his breakfast was placed before him and he discovered there was a price to pay, albeit only in kind.

Without preamble, the woman started in right away to dig for dirt, asked: 'Hear you got yourself mixed up in some trouble at Paul and Peg Calherns' place last night, mister?'

Edge answered evenly, with a quiet smile: 'Seem to recall I managed to keep clear of most of it.'

She said with a disdainful sniff: 'Well, yes. I'll tell you, if it was you shot dead Mr Mitchell, you wouldn't be welcome to have your feet under my table right now, mister.'

She folded her arms across her ample bosom, looked at him like she expected him to ask her to explain. When he remained silent, except for eating sounds, she went on:

'I don't really approve of mixed marriages, colour to another colour like. Especially when the man and the woman ain't been properly joined in the eyes of God. But I got a livin' to make and Mr Mitchell told me him and the woman were plannin' on stayin' in Ross awhile, if his luck with the cards ran good for him.'

'Lady, I——' Edge started.

'I ain't sayin' nothin' against breeds as such,' Maud Grogan hurried on, a glint of satisfaction in her flesh-crowded eyes now she had stirred a reaction in her reluctant audience of one. 'And I ain't just sayin' that because I heard how you beat up on Edward Noon for the way he insulted breeds. But I happen to believe we're all entitled to our own opinions. But some folks just don't think before they talk.'

'Lady, I—— Edge tried again.

Maud Grogan pulled a distasteful face, but hastened to explain she was not aiming the look at Edge. 'That Edward Noon, folks are real sick of how he struts around this town like he owns it! When all he owns, if truth was told, is the Golden Eagle: on account of the amount of money he's put over the bar at the Calherns' place...'

She shook her head in self-annoyance. 'Well, mister, I reckon what I'm tryin' to say is that if you want to beat up on me for speakin' my mind, then it's up to you. But I want you to know I approve right well of you takin' that swaggerin' loud-mouth down a peg or two?'

Edge had started to shovel down the food faster, enjoying it despite himself and his dislike for the woman who cooked it. When he became aware she had left him a pause, was waiting for a response, he told her with his mouth full:

'I agree everyone's entitled to their own opinions, lady. Just that sometimes people air them at a time and place that rubs me up the wrong way. This morning, I don't feel in any mood to beat up on anybody.'

He showed her another quiet smile, but the glittering slits of his eyes got colder rather than failed to convey warmth when he added: 'Even if they call a spade a nigger, maybe.'

'I'm glad to hear it, mister,' she said quickly, in a dismissive manner that suggested she had not actually heard what he told her. 'And there's somethin' else I'd be glad to hear. Is it true Vincent Mitchell really put up his woman as a hundred dollar bet?'

'You heard that?' Edge asked, not wanting to get on the wrong side of the woman before he had finished the fine breakfast, washed it down with another cup of her good coffee.

She nodded eagerly. 'From Ray, mister. I sent him down to the saloon after you come back here to your room. Seems half the town was there, findin' out why the shot got fired, why Craig Craven—that's the Ross undertaker—was out and about with his hearse so late. Way Ray and me fitted it together from what Ray was told, Mr Mitchell betted his common law wife when his money run out. And them other three strangers to town took him for all the money and his woman, too.'

'Way it happened,' Edge confirmed, mildly surprised to learn Harper, Wyler and Singer were not local men.

'You know where they went, mister?' Maud Grogan asked avidly.

'Who?'

She frowned her impatience at him, but abruptly recognised

such an attitude would gain her nothing. She asked in a tone that sounded just a little strained: 'That Harper and his two friends and the woman they won? Seems after Norris Pascall—he's the law in this country—was satisfied it was the first man to draw was killed, they went straight on back to the place they were camped in the timber. Packed up and left.'

Edge rattled the knife and fork on his empty plate, said: 'I'm much obliged for a fine breakfast, ma'am.'

He decided that what was left of his coffee would be sufficient to settle the food well enough in his stomach and raised the cup, finished it at a swallow.

'So you won't tell me nothin' else about last night that Ray didn't come home with at second hand?' She made no attempt to mask her irritable disappointment.

'No, ma'am.'

'Men!' She scowled as she rose suddenly from the table, reached across to snatch up his plate and cutlery. 'You're all the same. You just don't make the least effort to look at what's beyond the ends of your noses most of the time. Why, I bet if——'

'Be careful who you bet against around here,' Edge cut in. 'It could turn out to be your life that's in the pot.'

'If ever I need your advice, I'll ask for it, mister.'

'Like you do for hot gossip?' Edge countered as he got up less forcefully from the table. 'Like I said, the grub was fine. I'm real sorry I couldn't trade you any tasty food for thought for it. Morning to you, ma'am.'

'It's a small town!' she called defensively after him as he left the kitchen. 'When somethin' happens here, it's only natural that folks——'

He was outside the house and heard no more of what the disgruntled woman had to say. The essence of which he had anyway heard many times before from excitement-starved people in other small towns.

Joel Washington was not such an early riser as the couple who ran the boarding house. But he did not lock the doors of his premises, so Edge was able to get to his gelding in the stable at the western end of Ross's narrower street, next door to the blacksmith's forge and across from a dentist's office and a hardware store. None of these, nor any of the commercial businesses and houses he ambled between on the way from the Grogan place to the livery, showed signs of life. Except for wisps of smoke above some chimneys, rising from the embers of died-down fires waiting to be stirred into fiercer life for the new day.

But it was a Sunday morning, and it seemed that even in a town like Ross, where Saturday nights were not of the rip-roaring kind, the local population regarded the next day as one of rest.

Before Edge led his bay gelding out of the stable he carefully checked the animal over. Then he ensured that the sparse contents of his saddlebags were as he had left them, the action of the Winchester in the saddleboot worked smoothly and everything was as it should be in his bedroll.

The horse was in fine shape and nobody had interfered with his gear.

As at the Grogans, he had paid in advance for stabling services so he was all set to leave. Outside the livery he pushed a booted foot into the stirrup and made to swing up into the saddle. Had a clear conscience about leaving Ross, where he had paid his way. Felt satisfied by how he had earned more than enough by simply watching a hand of cards to cover the cost of the necessities and luxuries he had enjoyed here. Plus he could mentally cross this town off a non-existent list of places which he might find appealing enough to try settling down in.

'Mister!' a man called huskily as Edge hooked a hand around the saddlehorn.

He froze, identifying from the single word the tone of a black mood before he recognised the voice of the man when he warned:

'I can't let you get away with what you did to me!'

It was Eddie Noon who made the threat, getting greater force into his voice as he stood in the mouth of the alley between the office building and the Embury Hardware Store.

Edge got this bearing on the man's position before he let go of the saddlehorn, lowered his left foot and turned to put his

44

back to the horse without releasing the reins. So he did not need to seek out and find the tall, powerfully-built, thickly-moustached man who now emerged from the alley behind a horse trough on the other side of the fifty feet wide street.

'You can't?' the half-breed asked evenly, and noted that the belt with the ornate buckle had been replaced by a gunbelt with a revolver butt jutting out of the holster on the right side. Next he saw that the jaw beneath the carefully shaped moustache was swollen on one side, discoloured to a painful looking shade of purple.

Noon said: 'You're a driftin' saddletramp who's been around, that's plain to see, Edge.'

Now that he had overcome his initial nervousness he was enunciating his words carefully: to mask his emotions or because he was still drunk, or hungover.

'So?'

'So... Hell, would you be able to leave somethin' like that lay like it fell? And still be able to look at yourself in the mirror without throwin' up every time you shaved?'

Edge was aware of noise and movement off to his right along the street on which houses predominated over business premises. Creaking doors and whispering voices. Some footfalls. But he did not detect menace in the small sounds as the grey light of dawn was brightened by the first rays of sunlight from above the high ridges of the Cascades in the south east.

The new day's sun cast long shadows toward Noon as he moved away from the mouth of the alley, angling to his left to come around the side of the horse trough.

'I don't know, feller.'

'Sure you friggin' know!' Noon broke in before Edge could finish what he started.

The half-breed completed: 'Maybe if I knew I'd done something real stupid and deserved the beating I got for it, I might be able to do that.'

He directed a fast glance along the street and saw some doors were cracked open, some curtains were held aside. But he could only sense, rather than see, watching eyes.

'Shit, you jumped me when I wasn't lookin' and——'

'I know what I did,' Edge broke in, impatience hardening his tone. 'I was there. And I've just been over last night with somebody else. Be much obliged if you'd allow me to leave this town without causing me more trouble.'

Noon halted near one end of the trough, so it was still between him and Edge and sunlight reflected on the water threw bright patterns up on to his scowling face.

'Causin' you trouble?' he blurted. 'I got to live here, mister! I got to be able to hold my head up when I walk down the street, go into the Golden Eagle for a drink. I got——'

'Something you've got is the same as everyone else, feller,' Edge interrupted him again as Noon stepped around in front of the trough. 'You've got life. And like everyone else you're going to die from having it. Sooner or later.'

'I don't have the time to listen to all this crap!' Noon snarled, anger making him rigid from head to toe. Which was not a good attitude to adopt in any kind of fight.

Edge told him evenly: 'If you want it to be sooner in your case, you know how to fix it.'

'Uh?' He flexed the fingers of his gunhand while all the other muscles in his tall and broad frame seemed to be locked into immobility.

'You heard what I told Mitchell in the saloon last night. This morning, all you have to do is look like you're going to pull that gun on me. And I'll oblige you. Your head'll be hanging down, I guess, but you won't be concerned about that.'

'Noon! Stranger! Quit this stupidity right now!'

The voice, from a hundred feet away to the right of Edge, held a strident note of authority. And as he saw Noon snatch a look along the street, he guessed the man who gave the order was Norris Pascall. The county sheriff, who had been satisfied that Mitchell died in a fair gunfight, but did not sound like he was going to countenance any more gunplay of any kind in Ross.

'This is private business, Norris!' Noon yelled, and again showed his inexperience as a gunfighter by the way he once more turned his head to look away from Edge, toward the man he was addressing.

46

Edge reflected for a moment on whether he should take advantage of the basic error. If he could justify to himself drawing first on the grounds that Noon was at least fifteen years his junior, so might make up in speed of reflexes for what he lacked in the knowledge he would have gained from experience.

But he rejected such a course of action: continued to stand as before. Facing across the street, reins of the gelding in his left hand, his right hanging lower than the holstered sixgun, fingers slightly curved ready to fist around the butt and draw. Said without making a move:

'Private business that Noon figures has to be settled on a public street, Sheriff. So everyone can see what a hotshot he is. And will know that last night he was just unlucky.'

Having goaded Noon to a fresh height of anger, Edge now turned his head toward the lawman. But he did not direct his gaze in that direction. Which Noon failed to realise, since he was facing toward the newly-risen sun which did not reach Edge's eyes in the shadow under his Stetson brim.

And, just like Edge had planned, Noon went for his pearl-handled, plated revolver. With an action that was awkward as he sacrificed smoothness for speed, in a way that caused haste to produce the opposite of the desired effect. Noon was slow enough, even, for Edge to have the time to consider his options again.

For while the half-breed drew with the fluid speed of long experience, utilised reasonable fear of death or injury and their consequences as a steadying factor, he was able to make what was virtually a considered decision.

Whether to merely wing Noon or kill him. Alter his aim from the shoulder above the gun hand of the man to his chest, left of centre. Justify the end result with the contention that a man like this one would never let anything be, if he was seen to come off second best. Would always make the time and take the trouble to forget all other considerations so he could seek out his enemy and try yet again to even the score. Repeat what he was doing this morning after his humiliation of last night.

Edge squeezed the trigger of his Frontier Colt as the muzzle of Noon's fancier sixgun came clear of the holster, its hammer

47

thumbed back but the barrel not yet levelled.

The shot cracked out and acrid muzzle smoke spurted into the bright, clear, timber-scented morning. Then Noon's gun sounded an echoing report, fired by the hand of a dead man in the final second while his muscles held him up on his feet after his brain ceased to function.

Then, as the bullet drilled into the hard-packed dirt at his feet, puffing up dust, he fell backwards, hit the water trough with his legs and made to sprawl across it. But his rump splashed into it and the whiplash effect of the abrupt stop threw his head back, then jerked it foward. Where it hung down on his chest.

Even before the corpse had settled into the undignified posture and blood from the bullet hole in his chest had begun to stain the water, Edge had upended the Colt, pushed open the loading gate and used the ejector rod to push the still hot cartridge case out of the reeking chamber.

A shocked silence had gripped this part of town, unobtrusively broken by a distant clop of hooves and rattle of wheelrims from the south side of Ross as a wagon rolled southward on the trail to California.

Then the initial mass numbed response to early morning gunfire was ended and the stillness was shattered by shouted questions, running footfalls, doors and windows being opened with greater force than before.

As the impassive-faced Edge took a fresh round from a loop on his gunbelt and reloaded the Colt, he imagined he could still hear the far off progress of the wagon against the barrage of sound nearby. He guessed the rig had left the sawmill of the McAllister Lumber Company beside the trail a quarter mile beyond where the Golden Eagle Saloon and the church flanked the end of Ross's main street. And along with the sounds, he conjured up an image of Ray Grogan driving the team: a good breakfast inside him and now temporarily free of the domineering, far from beautiful wife who had cooked it for him. Not rich in many things other than money, nor possessing a perfect style of life. But happy enough for a proportion of the time: never having to wonder where the next dollar, the next meal or the next contented night's sleep was coming from.

Then, as Edge continued to stand across the street from the dead man sitting in the trough filled with crimson-stained water, slid the killing gun back in his holster and came close to envying another man, he was aware of somebody striding purposefully toward him. And sensed bristling anger before he turned to look at the sheriff. When it seemed like he could read precisely what was in the mind of Norris Pascall.

For on the sallow-skinned face of the fifty-years-old man with piercing grey eyes and a thin-lipped mouth there was the kind of scowl that starkly conveyed the rage of frustration. This man, six feet tall and not quite lean enough to be termed skinny, knew he had to do the right thing, even though he detested doing it: from the evidence of his own eyes and ears knew that as a peace officer he could not follow his instincts as a man.

'I see you got your horse already saddled and ready to ride, mister,' the lawman said as he angled from the centre of the street, stopped six feet in front of Edge.

'Just like you saw everything that happened here, Sheriff,' the half-breed replied to the man who was hurriedly dressed in pants, partly fastened shirt and unlaced boots, packed a sixgun pushed under a belt at his belly.

'Right,' Pascall agreed tautly, spread a harsher scowl across his disgruntled features. 'So I got to allow there's nothin' more I can do except tell you to get on your horse and ride out of this town.'

In back of the lawman, the throng of people disturbed by the shootout was expanding rapidly. They emerged from the buildings along this street, or came up on to the intersection from the main one that led out on to the south trail.

Edge nodded, swung smoothly up into his saddle without hindrance now as the crowd of hurriedly dressed Ross citizens advanced on this end of the street.

'I'm much obliged, Sheriff,' he said, aware that some of the local population seemed fascinated by the sight of him, his demeanour so calm after he had killed a man.

But they all carefully veered away from where he sat his

horse, Sheriff Pascall standing nearby. Headed instead for the water trough where the corpse no longer seeped blood out of the hole in its chest.

'You're a lot of things, none of them welcome in this town,' Pascall growled, his tone a match for his scowl.

'No sweat, this town doesn't have anything for me,' the half-breed answered.

Pascall spat out of the side of his mouth, accused: 'You didn't have to kill him.'

Edge shrugged. 'You got your opinion and I got mine, Sheriff.'

'Eddie Noon was full of hot air, mister. I could've cooled him down if I was given the chance. He couldn't shoot worth a damn, but you had to needle him into drawing against you.'

Edge pursed his lips, admitted: 'Yeah, I had to. It was a matter of pride.'

'You got nothing to be proud of, mister, way I see it.'

'Noon's pride,' Edge corrected.

'You don't give that much, do you?' Pascall sneered, and clicked a thumb and finger. 'About shooting down a man didn't stand a chance against somebody like you?'

The half-breed nodded, answered evenly: 'I sure don't give a shit Noon's pride came before my fall from grace.'

4

Rancour was almost a palpable presence in the sunlit morning air that now smelled only of woodsmoke as Edge rode down half the length of the cross street, then turned south, toward the far off California line.

The eyes that gazed fixedly at him showed undisguised condemnation for what had happened to Eddie Noon and he felt certain he could read the kind of thinking that generated this brand of dislike for him.

Noon had been the local braggart, but he was harmless. He had never done anything to anybody outside of riling them when he got drunker than he usually did on a Saturday night. Universally disdained, but nonetheless a local man. A son of Ross who deserved better than to end up with his dead ass in a water trough on a bright spring Sunday morning. Shot down by a sinister-looking, cold-eyed, passing-through stranger who flaunted a sixgun on his hip and looked like he did not have a good deed in him.

Of course, Edge could not know for sure if this was the line of anybody's thinking as they watched him ride a half length of one street, the full length of the other. But as he headed his horse between the saloon and the church and out on to the open trail, he figured that he was not too far wide of the mark with the surmise.

For he had heard similar things said about him in enough small towns not unlike this one in the Oregon timber.

Towns, maybe, where he would have liked to settle down if the circumstances had been right for it. And become an adopted son of the community. Where he would never be like Noon, or Ray Grogan or...

51

Or anybody, Goddamnit! He would always be himself, with as many faults as some people, probably fewer virtues than most.

But where he would belong. And where, in the event of an outsider causing him trouble, he would have the townspeople on his side. Not actively helping him if it was the kind of trouble in which lead might fly, maybe. But in spirit.

And if he should die, violently or from a natural cause, there would be people there who had known him for long enough and well enough to mourn his passing.

He mouthed an obscenity, spat more forcefully than had Sheriff Pascall, cursing himself for allowing his mind to lurch along this morbid line on such a fine Sunday morning as he left the grim little town of Ross behind him.

He reacted in this way as he rode past the gated entrance of the McAllister Lumber Company, where an old-timer sat out front of a small shack, smoking a pipe, drinking coffee and basking his leather-textured face in the morning sun.

'You mind tellin' me what the shootin' was in town, young feller?' the lumber company watchman called, and obviously it was shortsightness rather than his seventy-some years of living which made him refer to the half-breed as young.

'Yeah, I mind,' Edge growled as he rode on by the sawmill entrance with just a fleeting glance at the man slumped on a chair before the shack on the other side of the gates.

'Well, you can go to hell, you miserable sonofabitch!' the old man snarled back.

'Been a lot of places I'd guess are a lot like it, feller,' Edge answered, probably not loud enough for his voice to carry to the watchman. 'Looking for somewhere better now.'

Then he made a conscious effort to erase from his mind any kind of reflection on the painful past or wishful thoughts about a brighter future as he rode without haste along the trail that rose and fell, first curved one way then the other through a once densely forested area which was now patchworked where many sections of timber had been felled by the McAllister Lumber Company.

He stayed on the main trail that led inexorably southward

despite its many swings in other directions. Ignored the spurs that cut off to areas of felled timber on either side, in which the deep wheelruts and churned-up earth witnessed how teams had struggled to haul heavily laden lumber wagons through the worst kinds of weather, back to the sawmill at Ross.

As he moved through the fine Oregon country, by turns enclosed by densely growing trees on either side, then getting distant vistas in many directions from hillcrests where the elements or the destructive hand of man had stripped the land of timber, he endeavoured to find contentment in the sights and sounds and smells of the forested mountainscape.

But he doubted he could achieve this.

There were few parts of the United States and Territories where he had not ridden trails that cut through spectacular scenery, took him past many natural wonders. Often, he had to allow, when even if he were the kind of man to see beauty in a landscape for beauty's sake, he had been disinclined to take note of it. Because circumstances forced him to think of more mundane considerations, like his survival.

But he had never, anyway, developed that kind of sensitivity to his surroundings, good or bad, while he was required by events to exist where the whim of destiny or the need to raise a dollar had taken him. And it had always been an advantage that he could eat, sleep, make love or kill against whatever backdrop there happened to be, in the worst as well as some of the best of places.

And now he had taken the conscious decision to turn his back on that kind of life, he felt sure it was too late to try to develop any kind of affinity for the wonder of nature. So he would never choose where to put down new roots because of some breathtaking view of rolling hills, rushing rivers, rearing mountains or everchanging ocean. The place where one day he would make his home might equally well be among close-packed buildings lining crowded streets filled with the sights and sounds and smells of the city.

He could only hope that when he found it, he would recognise it as the place. Which was a risky way for a man to plan for the rest of his life. But it was his way and he knew of no

53

other: had survived for almost half a century by following his instincts. How much happiness such a way of living his life had gotten him was not something he was prepared to get into.

By midday, when he paused, he had ridden far beyond the southern extent of the lumber company's operation and was relishing the sense of isolation he drew from this knowledge.

He ate cold out of his saddlebags, the stale food unappetising but adequate after the fine breakfast Maud Grogan fixed for him. His bay gelding, a relatively new purchase after he was forced to shoot his wounded horse in Winton—another town which had not appealed to him—fared better by equine standards than he did: grazed on succulent spring grass on the bank of a clear, slow-running creek.

The afternoon was much like the morning, except that the new-found sense of being so completely detached from his fellow man was not so strong. And it irked him.

Because he was the kind of man circumstances had made him, he constantly looked about him, saw the beauty of his surroundings only in a peripheral way while he sought to detect a threat before it materialised. And since it was unavoidable, he also saw the signs that showed other people were moving down the trail ahead of him.

There was a wagon hauled by a four-horse team, ridden by two men: one who smoked a pipe, the other cigars. This would be the lumber company rig driven by Ray Grogan. Not a heavy wagon and certainly not one laden with timber, for the tracks of the wheels were not deep on the grassy areas where Grogan had twice called a halt to eat and rest.

There were also clear to see signs that three saddlehorses were being ridden southward. One of them had a broken shoe on the nearside hind hoof. One of the riders was a cigarette smoker, another chewed tobacco.

Edge looked no further than this, for it was purely an academic exercise after he recognised that he was a considerable distance behind the other travellers on the trail. But he could not help but register the sign, like other people noticed that the sun was shining, that a bird was perched on a branch or that a neighbour had started to build a new barn.

It was late in the afternoon but the sun was still bright and coloured yellow when he rode around an outcrop of rock on a hillcrest, and for the first time since he left Ross saw something he could not instantly forget because it was of no concern to him.

Because the people camped halfway down the gentle slope into a long valley stretching southward meant he had to make a decision. Whether to continue riding the trail, or to make a wide detour through the virgin forest: avoid one of the two groups of travellers he had known were moving south ahead of him.

He did not consider the alternatives just because he had had his fill of other people for awhile. There was a better reason than this for him to contemplate taking the time and trouble to ride around the night camp which had been set up so early.

For he could now see it was not three riders he had been following all day: acknowledged his mistake without any form of self-rebuke. For they rode only three horses and he had never felt any necessity to look closely enough at the hoofprints to see that one animal was carrying a double burden. Nor to search for any sign of a fourth traveller at the points where they rested. A fourth member of the group who was a woman.

She was instantly recognisable over a distance of a half mile from the hillcrest to the camp because of the combination of her blonde hair, red shirt, floral skirt and battered hat that hung down her back by the neckstrap around her throat. And once he recognised Ruby Red, it was then easy to differentiate between the grey-haired Prentice Harper, the fleshy Cecil Wyler and the emaciated Seymour Singer.

The men sat on one side of a newly laid fire just beginning to give off smoke, their horses hobbled on the other side. While Ruby Red squatted a little way off, peeling vegetables and tossing them into a pot.

The woman was not shackled by any physical restraints as far as Edge could tell from such a distance. And there was nothing in her attitude as she prepared the evening meal to suggest she undertook the chore against her will.

There was even, he thought after watching the scene for

55

more than a minute, some good-natured banter between Ruby Red and the three men who were engaged in another card game, using a flat-topped boulder for a table.

In fact, the half-breed allowed as he swung down from his saddle, it was an idyllic scene of peace and contentment as three totally relaxed men took their ease while a woman willingly prepared an evening meal for them. And maybe if he had not witnessed how this woman joined these men, Edge might have been persuaded by the domesticity of the scene to ride openly down the trail, introduce himself to the people at the camp, expect them to extend to a stranger the hospitality of their camp, as was customary among innocent travellers on the frontier.

But he did know how this woman came to be with these men, so he was aware that all was not as it seemed. And since he was familiar with the kind of people who comprised the group, he found himself presuming that the choice of the campsite was not a random one.

It was a hundred feet off the trail to the west, in a small clearing exposed to view from the hilltop where Edge stood beside his horse, absently stroking the animal's neck as he swept his gaze the length and breadth of the valley which stretched several miles southward, the trail to California following the long curves of a stream that had its source at the foot of this hill.

From his higher vantage point, Edge could not see if the campsite commanded a similar but truncated view down the valley. But it was clear that Harper and his partners and their newly-acquired female companion could have, from the top of the hill, seen at least a score of places more suitable for a night camp. Along the valley bottom, close to the fresh water in the stream, hidden from watching eyes once the need of a fire had passed.

And since the sun only now began to take on a reddish hue as it eased down on the south-western horizon and the camp had obviously been pitched some time ago, urgency could not have been a factor in calling the halt here.

But, Edge allowed with a grunt, maybe the place was chosen simply because it took their fancy at a time of day when they had all had enough of being in the saddle since early morning. They were four free agents, drifting through the Oregon mountains and forests, three looking for another card game to strengthen their joint stake, the woman going where the luck of the draw of life took her. Not one of them with the experience or the plain commonsense to pick any of many better places available for a night camp. So they had settled for the first one they happened upon . . .

Edge now rasped a soft-spoken curse as Seymour Singer threw down his hand of cards, rose from where he squatted beside the flat top rock. But it was not the move by the tall and thin man in the out of fashion city suit that triggered a reaction from Edge. It was a sound of self-rebuke.

For it was no concern of his why the four men and a woman were camped where they were, he told himself with a scowl as he watched the skinny man go around the fire to the woman, say something to her. It should not matter to him if they were truly innocents abroad, drifting where the fancy took them or if . . .

Over a distance of a half mile, as the sun turned completely red and its leading arc touched the horizon, Edge was unable to discern the slightest hint of reluctance in the way Ruby Red interrupted her chore, extended a hand so Singer could help her to her feet. Then she walked behind him, without any further physical contact, to the side of the clearing, while the other two men continued to play cards. They did not even look up from the card game and Edge found himself wondering, with another scowl fixed firmly to his features, how often one of the men had demanded the submissive services of the woman during the day.

He tried to convince himself he felt shame as he watched the man and the woman, not hidden from the card players if they elected to look, clearly visible from the top of the hill in the fading light.

Peg ain't never allowed no loose women in our place, Edge heard repeated in memory as he found himself compelled to gaze fixedly at what was taking place: tried to tell himself he experienced no emotion.

Ruby Red is no whore! he heard Vincent Mitchell's voice

counter the accusation of the Ross saloonkeeper.

But she was sure acting like a whore now: complied without protest to the orders of a man who had been a stranger to her this time yesterday. One of three men who had been such strangers, Edge was forced to acknowledge as an acidly rancid taste suddenly rose out of his throat, and he told himself this was caused by the awful midday meal mixing with the good home cooking of Maud Grogan.

Seymour Singer stopped and turned to lean his back against a pine trunk. Took out a plug of tobacco. Said something to the woman who immediately went down on her knees before him. Singer bit off a chew of tobacco as she reached out both hands to unfasten his belt buckle, then fly buttons.

Next, without revulsion or passion, her movements as calmly deliberate as when she had been preparing supper, Ruby Red eased his pants down his skinny thighs and caressed him briefly with her hands. Until he hooked both his hands around the back of her head and she dropped her arms to her sides, took him into her mouth.

Edge wrenched his gaze away from the couple then, and felt no kind of taste in his own mouth. Instead, experienced in his throat a brand of almost palpable sound that he was sure would explode free of his compressed lips, roar from this end of the valley to the other if he continued to watch: even did not direct his mind to something outside of what the woman was doing to the man. The man not forcing himself upon the woman who Edge had found strangely attractive in a situation when she had been as unattainable as now.

He drew back, along the side and then behind the outcrop of granite, to place a solid barrier between himself and the scene below. But it was not so easy to rid his mind's eye of the vivid image as he hitched the reins of his horse to a low branch of a tree, leaned his back against the rock and dug for the makings. Was aware his hands shook a little as he carefully rolled and lit a cigarette, blew out a stream of smoke and told himself he was reacting like an asshole.

He was not looking for women.

Women were readily available in the right places if a man

was not looking for a particular one.

And if he were to find a place where he could settle down, the kind of woman that Ruby Red obviously was would never be anything other than a female body on which to relieve frustration. In the manner she was serving the lustful purpose of Singer, or in any other way a whore was willing to sell herself.

He half smoked the cigarette as the red light of the setting sun extended from the far west to halfway across the heavens, met with the darkness encroaching from the east. Only then was able to think of something other than the half-breed woman: be she satisfying the sexual desires of another man or staring at him with the kind of pleading she had conveyed to him in the Golden Edge Saloon last night.

And in the gathering darkness of night crowding out twilight, he was able to reach a logical conclusion about why Harper had picked a particular place to make night camp so early in the day. And it would be Harper who made the decision, he felt certain, for he was the undisputed leader of the bunch.

They had been strangers in Ross who had broken camp and left town early, he had been told without asking by Maud Grogan. And Edge had then been inclined to think of them as opportunists who got lucky, happened to meet up with a gambling fool who was also a passing-through stranger.

By luck, judgement or maybe Mitchell was right and cheating had played a part, they had collected a bundle of bucks and the company of a half-breed woman who perhaps lacked beauty but was experienced in supplying what every red-blooded man required from time to time.

Maud Grogan, who endeavoured to find out everything there was to know about events in Ross, had not said the men had left because the strong-willed but fair-minded sheriff had ordered them out of town. Like he certainly would have done if Harper had gunned down a local man in a similar situation.

So why had the men with their newly-acquired woman companion left the vicinity of Ross so early? And made only slow progress down the south trail?

At some time during the day they would have been overhauled by the McAllister Lumber Company wagon driven by Ray Grogan who had somebody riding with him.

Had there been a passing of the time of day between the men aboard the wagon and the horseback riders? Or had the Harper bunch purposely avoided being seen?

The wagon could have rolled on down the trail during one of many times when the men had taken the woman into the timber to enjoy her as the fruits of victory in...

Edge took the cigarette out of his mouth, cursed softly again and spat into the darkness relieved by moon and starlight. Maybe these were not ordinary men by the standards of the kind who lived in Ross, for instance. But they were mere men. And their capacity for screwing was governed by the basic laws of human sexuality.

Also, Harper, Singer and Wyler were men of the world: no strangers to drifting around the frontier towns of the west. And having ready access to a woman of easy virtue was no novelty.

So Edge reached the conclusion there was a sound reason why this group headed up by a cool-thinking, intelligent man like Prentice Harper was dragging its feet on the ride south. And had chosen to call a halt for the night so early, halfway down a hillside at the head of a valley.

By instinct, intuition, a gut feeling, or whatever else caused a man to have a hunch, Edge was certain this bunch were up to no good. Further, he felt sure their plans were somehow connected with the departure of the McAllister Lumber Company wagon from Ross early this Sunday morning. Sunday was not a usual working day and the wagon did not carry any of the usual stock in trade of the company. Which maybe meant...

Beyond this, Edge was not prepared to delve into the realm of conjecture. Because by now there was no further need to flood his mind with conjured-up lines of thought to blot out stark images of reality.

Night was full born and the native creatures of the timber country were making themselves heard more forcefully than in the daytime, like the night air held a quality that gave extra clarity to sound. A distant wolf, an owl that was in the trees much closer, even the tiny living things of the forest floor, made themselves heard distinctly as they went about their business of seeking out whatever it was they needed to survive. Many of them predators, the others prey.

Edge had been at the side of the rock for perhaps an hour when he straightened up and moved forward to look down the hillside again. Saw that the entire valley was a black mass under the moonlight, except for the sparkling river, the pale strip of trail beside it and the red glow of the fire at the campsite below him.

The fire had obviously blazed while supper was cooked, was now allowed to die down, its heat not needed and its light perhaps dangerous to whatever the men had in mind.

He could smell the woodsmoke, and was grateful he had not caught the aroma of the food Ruby Red had cooked. For that meant it was easier to squat down and eat a supper as unappetising as the midday meal had been without envying the men down the hillside.

The night that fell while he was forcing his mind to think along lines that barred other notions made it difficult to get around the camp below without the people there being alerted that somebody was nearby. Unless he were to swing into a wide, time-consuming detour which took him beyond earshot of the three men and a woman.

But he knew it would be no hardship to stay where he was for the night. And despite being a little riled at himself for his curiosity—he was not prepared to admit it was anything other than this that triggered his interest—he felt a compelling need to see how things were going to turn out.

And if nothing of any consequence happened, well ... All he had lost an hour or so of daylight travelling time. And he had foregone the opportunity of ready access to the fresh water from the stream and some hot food cooked on a fire that would have been possible had he pressed on, made camp way off down the valley.

But, he rationalised, the water in his canteens was still pretty fresh, taken from another mountain stream not so many hours ago. And he could get by on the basic chow he had eaten without suffering malnutrition. Sleep without a fire and not freeze to death among these low mountain tops in the spring time of the year.

And, anyway, he had spent so damn long trying to convince himself he was pausing here out of mere curiosity, it was now too late to have any other option.

So what if bedding down under the stars in a remote piece of country not of his choosing was no longer any part of the kind of life he was looking to make for himself? Experience of doing just this so often in the past meant he could handle its minor discomforts without ill effect.

And as a bonus it also served to delay yet again the time when he would come face to face with options he knew he would have to choose between for good and honest reasons: or forever regret the lost opportunity.

He knew as he stooped to unfasten the cinch beneath the belly of the gelding that it was only a trick of the moonlight striking the animal's eye, but it certainly seemed like the horse gave him a cynically censuring look. And as he came upright and hauled the saddle off the back of his mount, he felt moved to rasp sardonically:

'Yeah, I know it. Curiosity's killed more than cats. And I guess a whole lot more men have gone down for pussy.'

5

Edge slept under the blankets from his bedroll on the spring pine needles which thickly covered the ground in back of the granite outcrop. Here, he and his horse were out of sight and earshot of the three men and a woman a half mile down the slope, and were also effectively concealed from anyone who might happen to pass along the trail during the hours of darkness.

But nothing happened in the night to disturb the half-breed's customary shallow level of sleep. And he awoke at sun-up feeling luxuriously rested: contented enough with his lot not to think for perhaps a full minute about the circumstances that had caused him to be bedded down in this particular spot.

During this time he remained sprawled on his back, his Stetson removed from his face. Consciously breathing the cool, crystal-clear, pine-scented morning air as he peered up at the patch of cloudless sky visible above the surrounding treetops and the slab of granite. Contemplated a future filled with such awakenings each day, untroubled by disconcerting memories, confident about facing up to the undemanding challenges he would meet during the day ahead.

Then his horse vented a low whinny, as if to call attention to the truth that a man could not live entirely for the gratification of self-interest: had responsibilities that must first be attended to if he wished to enjoy those simplest of pleasures that never did come free.

But as he felt a scowl of mild irritation grip his features, Edge became aware that the gelding was not asking for attention. Instead was giving unobtrusive vent to a nervous reaction as a new body of sound intruded on the quiet of the early morning.

This was the thud of galloping hooves and the rattle of wheelrims on hard-packed ground. The sounds coming from some way off to the south but rising steadily in volume as the fast-moving wagon headed northward.

And the final remnants of the half-breed's contentment were shredded to nothing, while the only confidence he now experienced was concerned with the hunch he had nurtured about a less than innocent reason for the camp being set up at a midway point down the hillside.

He quickly slid out from under his blankets, taking with him the Winchester rifle that had shared his bed. Jammed the Stetson hard on his head and spat out the taste of a night's sleep as he moved around the rock. Stepped onto the trail and went toward the brow of the hill from where he could survey the entire length of the valley.

He reached the vantage point just as the people in the camp were jerked from sleep by the same series of sounds that had ended his musings about his personal vision of the perfect life.

But in his world this early Monday morning, anything close to a state of perfection looked like it was as far removed from him as it invariably was.

He glanced for just a moment at the activity in the camp below, then shifted the direction and lengthened the focus of his narrowed eyes: peered along the valley and saw a wagon and two-horse team about a mile away. Heading northward on the curving trail beside the stream, the horses starting to slow as the driver hauled on the reins, getting ready for the less than steep but long and energy-draining climb out of the northern end of the valley.

Then Edge returned his gaze to the camp in the clearing off the trail some halfway down the slope. In time to see that although Ruby Red had been submissive while everyone was alert, she was not trusted to remain so co-operative during the night. And now, while Singer and Wyler attended to saddling their horses, Harper was crouched beside the woman, unfastening the knots of the ropes that bound her ankles together, her wrists behind her back.

There was a frenetic urgency about the activity at the camp, a tone of high tension in the harsh exchanges. The words were incomprehensible to Edge over the distance, but the meaning was plain: demands were made to hurry up and excuses returned that things were getting done as fast as they could be.

The short and flabby Cecil Wyler, his obese body straining his too-tight clothes, drew most of the criticism for his heavy breathing slowness. But the tall and slender Ruby Red came in for a share of censure after she was free of her bonds. Once Seymour Singer even lashed out at her with a fist, but she easily ducked under the clumsy swing, like an experienced prize fighter matched against a punchdrunk opponent.

'You bitch!' Singer yelled with shrill-voiced frustration.

And in turn was snarled at by Harper who clearly warned him about the nearness of the approaching wagon.

For a moment Edge considered staying where he was to watch the outcome of the hurried breaking of camp. What it meant in relation to the approaching wagon he was certain would be the McAllister Lumber Company rig making its return to Ross.

But he felt at a disadvantage without having his horse ready to ride. And figured he had enough time to break his own camp, saddle the gelding and be back in position to witness the climax of events in the valley without missing out on too much.

But not much more than a minute later it looked at first like he had made a mistake. That was how much time it took him to do what was necessary, to the disgust of the gelding who objected to the hurried saddling with a disgruntled snort.

For when he returned to the top of the hill, leading his mount by the bridle, only the slow-moving rig was in sight. Harper, Singer, Wyler and Ruby Red were no longer to be seen: just the remains of their fire showing where they had been camped in the clearing.

But what the hell did it matter to him, Edge asked himself as he became aware of another unbidden scowl stiffening his facial muscles, his thin lips drawing back from his teeth, his eyes narrowing to glittering slits of ice blue. It was now as dazzlingly plain to see as the sun in the south eastern sky that the Harper bunch planned to spring an unwelcome surprise on

Ray Grogan and his passenger—a man riding shotgun to protect the valuable payload?

And the finer details of how and precisely where the hold-up was to take place were no concern of his, Edge acknowledged as he took a tighter grip on the frame of the Winchester in one hand, the bridle in the other and came to the brink of venting a soft curse of irritation.

Then he spotted movement on the trail, way ahead of the wagon. Maybe a hundred feet back up the hill from where the camp had been, he saw Ruby Red move out from the trees and stand on the centre of the trail. Where she remained immobile for several seconds, peering back into the timber where she had emerged. Until she swung her head around to look in the opposite direction, like something had been said to her from this side of the trail.

There was anger in her attitude, like she was impatient with the final instructions that were given her.

Now Edge switched his gaze constantly between the woman and the wagon, until it went from sight under a canopy of trees through which the trail curved before the ground started to rise.

Then he concentrated his attention on Ruby Red: saw her anger had expanded as she threw up her hands and over the distance it seemed to him like she was going to claw at her own face or maybe try to throttle herself with her bare hands. But then she hooked her fingers inside the neckline of her shirt and jerked them down: wrenched it open to the waist as buttons popped and fabric ripped.

Immediately, just as the horses in the wagon traces came into sight out of the trees, slowly, to climb the hill, she sat down hard on the centre of the trail. Jerked her skirt up around her thighs and splayed her long legs. Threw her arms to the sides, thudded her back—and the back of her head—to the ground.

Plainly she was bitterly opposed to what she was being forced to do: uncaring that she caused herself physical pain by the force with which she conveyed her resentment. Or maybe she had tried to knock herself out by crashing her head against the hard-packed surface of the trail.

From where he stood beside his nervous horse, Edge had a

distant view of the bare-legged, naked to the waist, woman spreadeagled, on the trail. Had to force himself to look away from the powerfully erotic attitude she had assumed, switch the direction of his narrow-eyed gaze to the men up on the open seat of the enclosed wagon.

They were getting a much more startling view of Ruby Red's state of violent undress as the rig rolled closer to her. And whether because of sexual arousal at seeing her exposed legs and torso, or compassion for a seemingly injured fellow human being, the driver and his passenger riveted their attention on her.

Seemed suddenly immune to all else, which was surely what Harper, Singer and Wyler had intended.

But was the wagon going to stop? Edge was abruptly gripped by a degree of concern that caused him to let go of the bridle and take a two handed grasp on the Winchester. Which he angled across his chest, an instant away from bringing it to the aim from his shoulder.

Maybe the driver would stay too surprised for too long. Or else either man could figure the woman on the centre of the trail was a ploy. And a failure to react quickly enough or a decision to command a spurt of high speed from the team could have the same bone-crunching result for Ruby Red if she realised too late she had to lunge away from plunging hooves and spinning wheels.

But Ray Grogan—Edge recognised it was the stockily built man who had the reins—recovered from the shock of seeing the unmoving woman who blocked the trail. And had no trouble in bringing the team to a halt short of where she lay. For because of the slow speed on the upgrade of the trail the animals stopped immediately he hauled on the reins, jerked the brake lever so the blocks bit against the wheelrims.

Maybe Grogan and his taller, younger, black-moustached partner glanced fleetingly to left and right as the wagon came to a standstill, fearful of a trap, or able to sense all was not well, or to check if the attacker of the half-naked woman was still nearby. But it could only have been with a flicking of their eyes along the sockets. Over the intervening distance, it seemed to

Edge like both men stared with riveted fascination at Ruby Red for stretched seconds.

Then he saw them snap their heads from side to side: reacting to sounds that signalled they were not alone. Perhaps the crack of a dry twig under a booted foot, or more likely words that were snarled at them.

Grogan stared to the left, his passenger to the right. Then each swung his head to look in the opposite direction. And thrust their arms above their heads in response to a tacit or spoken command as Prentice Harper stepped out of the timber on the side of the trail where Ruby Red had come from, and Cecil Wyler and Seymour Singer emerged from the trees on the other side.

Each of the three men was masked by a kerchief that covered the lower half of his face and each carried a rifle, angled up at the two on the wagon seat.

Apart from when he was anxious that the wagon might not halt before running over the woman, Edge had watched the hold-up with an impassive expression on his heavily-bristled face that truly conveyed how he felt about what he was seeing.

He was satisfied with his hunches about this whole thing: that it was the lumber company wagon that interested the three men, and they had pitched their night camp precisely where they did so they were well positioned for its early morning approach, could easily stop it on a hill where it would be making slow progress as it emerged from around a curve through the timber and the first sight of the half-naked woman would not allow the driver and passenger any time to think about the possible dangerous ramifications of what they were seeing.

He was satisfied, but had no sense of elation at guessing the actions of Harper and the others in a situation such as this, when he had nothing to gain or lose from his foresight. Unless he counted the satisfying of his curiosity.

But now Edge found himself experiencing doubt again, and once more a scowl spread across his face. This as he watched the men with rifles close in on the wagon, Harper on the driver's side, Singer and Wyler the other. And Ruby Red got to her feet, the hem of her skirt falling to her ankles of its own accord as she clutched the torn-open shirt in front of her breasts.

The early morning stillness of the timber-cloaked mountainscape beyond the vicinity of the hold-up suddenly seemed menacingly brittle. Not at all like the tranquil peace that had reigned when he woke up, pleasant images filling his mind even though he was so sure something evil was being planned just a few hundred yards away.

But back then it had been easy to remain detached from what he had accurately predicted was going to happen. Now it was taking place, he found it was impossible to ignore what was happening: remain a bystander even though the trouble was no concern of his.

Because maybe it was, damnit!

If he were ever to have a stable life in a community among his fellow men, he had to adopt a more conventional set of moral standards than those he had lived by until now. And the most fundamental canon had to be a clear understanding of the difference between right and wrong. Especially in such a clearcut circumstance as this, when there was not even a grey area between the two, and a right-thinking man had to side with the wronged against the wrongdoers.

And a right-thinking man in a position to help the wronged should accept his responsibility and attempt to do just that. It didn't matter a damn whether he was directly involved or if there was no material gain to be had.

It took him just two or three seconds to consider this line of thought that would have gone so much against the grain not long ago. While he continued to watch the hold-up about halfway down the hill: decided by a sequence of coolly-reasoned thinking to take a hand.

When the time was right.

But then the impulsive actions of somebody else forced his hand.

The men on the wagon had been ordered to climb down from their seats, and this is what they started to do. And they should have completed doing as they were told if they had taken the time to think clearly about their situation. For the masks worn by the hold-up men signalled they had no intention of shooting down the lumber company men: planned only to rob the wagon and ride off, with no risk of being identified later.

From thinking this way, or out of a terrified inability to resist, Ray Grogan eagerly complied with the order. But his partner was either attacked by a bout of company loyalty or did not trust the masked men to stop short of cold-blooded murder. Or maybe he was needled by something somebody said.

Whatever the reason, instead of using both his hands, as Grogan did, to steady himself as he started to climb off the wagon, he shoved one inside his jacket: just had time to drag the butt of a revolver out from under a lapel before Prentice Harper's rifle exploded a shot at him.

The bullet cracked past Grogan and took the other man under the jaw, jerked his head back and sent him flying backwards off the wagon, blood gouting from his holed jugular vein. He was instantly dead and spasmed in mid-air, hit the ground like a loosely-packed sack of grain and settled into an untidy heap, arms and legs twisted at awkward angles.

If he had had the time to utter a vocal response to violent death it was inaudible to Edge against the scream of terror vented by Ray Grogan. Who froze in the act of getting down off the wagon, tightly gripping the seat rail with one hand while his other arm thrust high in the air, ramrod stiff.

The shrill cry caused all the rifles to swing to cover him.

Just as instinctively, Edge threw the butt of his Winchester to his shoulder. Drew a bead on Harper, thumbed back the hammer behind a live shell already in the breech, squeezed the trigger.

The range was long, the angle downwards, but his aim was true. The bullet tunnelled into Harper's chest, high and to the right: still had enough impetus to twist him and knock him off his feet, the rifle slipping out of his weakened grip.

Once more reacting from instinct, without taking a moment for calculated thought, both the tall and skinny Singer and the short and fat Wyler swung away from the wagon and its driver and Ruby Red. To look and aim their rifles in the direction from which the gunshot had cracked.

Edge, his ice-blue eyes narrowed to glittering threads and his lips drawn back from his teeth in the killer's grin that fitted so easily on his lean face, swung the lever action of the Winchester down and forward. Slapped it back into position to jack a fresh round out of the magazine, into the breach.

The expended shellcase was still arcing through the early morning air when he saw the puffs of white smoke from the muzzles of both men's rifles below him.

As he squeezed his trigger a second time he was aware on the periphery of his vision of a flurry of activity on the other side of the wagon to where Singer and Wyler stood.

Something red, moving fast. Red was the colour of the woman's shirt.

He had aimed at the shorter, fatter man because Cecil Wyler presented the easier target to hit over such a long range. And he made no move to avoid the two shots fired at him: knew there was no time to avoid being hit if either man were a crack shot, and that if they were relying on luck, he had as much chance of getting shot standing still as moving.

He heard one bullet ricochet off the outcrop of rock several feet to his left. Did not know if the other one came anywhere near him as he watched Wyler hurl away his gun, clutch at his belly and stagger backwards for several clumsy paces, screaming that he was hit.

By now, Singer had learned a fast lesson that it was dangerous to concern himself with what was happening nearby when a sharpshooter was exploding lethal gunfire from a distance. A sharpshooter who stood out in the open, starkly silhouetted against the bright morning sky.

He pumped the lever action of his repeater, drew a more careful bead on Edge: and found out the hardest way there is that he had made the wrong decision. For a bullet tunnelled into his back from short range, with enough velocity to send him into a staggering run. Until his dead hands released the rifle and his dead legs collapsed under him. And he pitched to the ground, probably had no time to even start to wonder what had happened to him, was maybe too shocked to experience any pain.

Edge had used the lever action of his Winchester in unison with Singer. But was able to check his trigger finger at first pressure when he heard the shot and saw its effect. Kept the rifle pressed to his shoulder as he shifted his gaze from the dead man he had not killed, to look fleetingly at the two he had shot.

Prentice Harper was unmoving and could be dead.

Cecil Wyler was sitting on the ground, short legs splayed out in front of him, pressing both hands to his stomach. But he was not able to staunch the flow of blood from his gut wound and it oozed out between his interlocked fingers.

He was in no condition to try to reach for his discarded rifle when he saw Ruby Red moving around the front of the horses in the wagon traces.

It was Harper's fallen rifle she had scooped up and used on Singer, firing from the hip. And she held it in the same position now, unmindful of the torn shirt that gaped open, flapping lethargically at either side of her naked breasts.

Edge thought he could see Cecil Wyler's fleshy lips moving as Ruby Red came to a halt six feet in front of him. Perhaps he pleaded with her as she angled the barrel down to aim at his face. Or maybe he taunted her when he stared into her dark eyes and realised that right then she was incapable of feeling pity, being merciful.

Whatever he said to the tall, slender, blonde-haired and dark-skinned half-breed, she blasted a shot between his eyes. And the impact of the bullet in his head sent him forcefully backwards, where he twitched once from head to toe, then was still.

Next, as Edge lowered his rifle and eased the hammer forward, Ruby Red turned away from the blood-run corpses of Wyler and Singer.

And Ray Grogan hurried to balance himself precariously with his feet on a front wheel of the wagon, his knees pressed against the side of the seat so he was able to push both arms high again.

But the terrified wagon driver was not a target for Ruby Red's spite. And she must have told him so, for he dropped his arms, scrambled back on to the seat and snatched up the reins. Then either she said something to him that caused him to delay leaving, or he became gripped by a brand of horrified fascination as he watched the woman move to where Prentice Harper lay.

Harper had not moved since he went down, a bullet in his chest. But that didn't have to mean he was dead. Edge was too far removed from the scene to see any slight rise and fall of the man's chest. And he thought that perhaps the woman was too emotionally involved in what she was doing to care, one way or the other, if she was ending Harper's life or if she was carrying out a mere symbolic act of revenge against the man who had won her in a card game, forced her to suffer the greater degradation of sharing her body with his friends.

But certainly Harper was not conscious as she advanced on him, stooped a little so she could press the muzzle of the Winchester into his crotch.

She pulled the trigger.

The horses in the wagon traces, which had shied and reared against their restraints at the earlier gunfire and the acrid stink of the black powder smoke, had become immune to this brand of violence now.

But Edge's gelding reacted as if this final distant shot had snapped the over-stretched nerve that had been strained to keep him calmly quiet for so long during the earlier exchange of gunfire.

The animal whinnied and Edge had time to throw down his rifle and grasp the reins in both hands as the gelding reared, taking the bridle out of reach. Entered into a battle of strength and wills with the gelding as he flailed his forelegs and snorted his mounting terror, eyes bulged, teeth bared, ears pricked and sweat lathering across his coat.

In countless other circumstances, the superior strength of the horse would certainly have triumphed over that of the man. The plunging, circling, shrieking animal would have wrenched the reins free of the man's hands: wheeled and bolted to put great distance between himself and the human kind which had caused his blind panic.

But Edge was possessed of a powerful will to win this contest with a dumb animal. And felt like his natural brute strength was increased many times by the self anger at having persuaded himself to take a hand in the carnage. By submitting to the compulsion, for whatever fanciful reasoning concerned with developing a social conscience, he felt like he had lost out: was somehow a weaker character than he was before. And he sure as hell wasn't going to lose this battle of a clear-thinking man against a terrified animal.

At first he used brute force along with a series of snarled obscenities that took the place of hurting the innocent horse with kicks, punches or even a killing gunshot.

Then, once the initial fear of the gelding was eased, the sounds of his terror silenced and he lost the urge to lash out with his hooves, Edge spoke softer words of persuasion to soothe the final traces of fight and fright out of the animal.

The battle was won, man and horse run with sweat. And as they started to recover their breath, seemingly unable to move an aching muscle, some of the dust kicked up during the struggle adhered to coat and skin. While a blessed silence came to the north end of the valley: maybe extended for many miles to the south and out across the mountains to the east and west. It certainly seemed to the deeply-breathing Edge like the entire world came to a stop for many stretched seconds.

Then he looked around, saw that the fight with the horse had drawn him back from the brow of the hill beside the rock outcrop. He led his mount back to where he had dropped the Winchester and took the time to reload the magazine. Slid the rifle back in the boot and swung gratefully up into the saddle. Rode to the crest of the hill and down on to the slope without pausing. Rolled a cigarette and hung it from the side of his mouth as he watched the changed and still slowly changing scene near the stalled wagon.

In no hurry to get down there, be faced again with the prospect of behaving like a man who had turned over a new leaf to become like other men.

In the time it had taken to calm the spooked horse, Ray Grogan had done the right thing by his partner. Only a stain of dried blood on the trail showed where the shot man had fallen from the wagon. There was a like-coloured stain on Grogan's shirt front as he moved from the rear of the wagon, climbed wearily up on to the seat, which suggested he had loaded the corpse aboard to bring back to Ross.

Ruby Red sat on her haunches off to the side of the trail, her back against a tree trunk. A rifle rested across her thighs and her head was bowed as one hand held her torn shirt together. Her attitude was of total physical exhaustion, and Edge guessed she had herself taken care of the corpses of Harper, Singer and Wyler. Had dragged them from where they dropped to place them in a neat line beside where she sat. By accident, or maybe because she wanted to look at their dead faces, the kerchiefs that had been masks were now around their necks. Two Winchesters and the revolver which had been dropped by Grogan's partner as he fell were together on the ground between Ruby Red and the line of bodies.

The half-breed woman did not look up after Edge rode close enough for the slow clop of hooves to be within earshot. Nor when he was recognised by the white-faced, no longer bright-eyed Grogan who called huskily:

'Boy, am I grateful to you, Mr Edge!'

'Wish I could tell you it was a pleasure, feller,' Edge replied flatly.

'But if you hadn't shown up and——'

'Don't think anything of it, uh?'

Grogan shook his head ruefully, swallowed hard and looked like he was close to being sick to his stomach before he admitted: 'Well, I reckon I'm goin' to be thinkin' about all of this a whole lot, Mr Edge. Likely wake up in a cold sweat over it a lot of nights. You wanna give me an address where you're gonna be?'

'What?' Edge interrupted the process of striking a match on the butt of the Colt that jutted from his holster.

'I need to know where you're headed so I can——'

'I won't know where that is until I get there,' the half-breed cut in. 'Even if that wasn't so, what——'

'Damnit, mister, you just saved the McAllister Lumber Company a big bundle of money.' The frowning Grogan jerked a hooked thumb over his shoulder to indicate the enclosed wagon he was driving. 'There's been some kinda delay in raisin' the payroll money for six weeks. Usually me and the rest of the guys get paid every week. But we all agreed to keep on workin' when the company said there'd be a bonus at the end of it.'

He had been talking fast and needed to take a long pause to draw breath. While he did this, Edge struck the match and lit the cigarette. Grogan went on with less frenetic haste:

'Reason me and Joe Biles snuck outta town early Sunday mornin'. And made a fast turnaround. Drove through the night. Told there'd be a little extra for us if hurried things up and the bonuses would be low as possible.'

Edge nodded, said: 'So you better be on your way to Ross, not waste any more time.'

Grogan nodded more emphatically, agreed: 'What I plan to do. But there's better than fifty thousand bucks aboard this wagon. And I reckon the company'll be grateful enough to come up with some kinda reward when they find out what you done so it didn't get stolen.'

Ruby Red vented a low growl of wearied scorn.

Grogan insisted: 'And since I figure you saved my skin, I plan to do what I can to make them come——'.

'He didn't do it on his own,' Ruby Red reminded dully.

Both men looked at her now, as she lifted her head and tossed it, to swing the long, dishevelled, blonde hair from off her face. And they saw in the haggardness of her features just how mentally and physically drained she was. But deep in the darkness of her eyes there was a glint of resolute determination as she stared into the middle distance.

Grogan nodded, looked and sounded nervous as he spluttered: 'Well, I don't know if the company'll pay more than the one reward. So what you two people do about splittin' it, that'll be up to you and I——'

'You get your shotgun rider loaded aboard yet?' Ruby Red

cut in, still gazing at infinity. And it was obviously not a rhetorical question. She had been completely withdrawn into a private world while she sat against the tree after dealing with three of the corpses. Now she was disinclined to take the trouble to look around for the body of Joe Biles.

'Yeah, I did that,' Grogan reported morosely.

'So you're ready to haul all that temptation out of my sight,' she murmured.

'Uh?'

'I didn't know there was that much money aboard when they made me help them with the hold-up, Mr Grogan,' Ruby Red told him. 'I didn't want no part of gettin' money that way. But I had to do like I was told or end up like this.'

She raised the hand off the rifle, waved it over the line of corpses, went on: 'But now I know how much you're carryin' and there wouldn't be no sharin' it with . . .' She pulled a face, gripped the rifle again but not in a menacing way. 'And since I've already killed two guys, one more won't make me lose any extra sleep. So best you be on your way, mister. Before I think too hard about it and figure I could get real hot over a cool fifty thousand.'

Grogan swallowed hard again, perhaps looked more frightened than at any time since the three masked men with rifles emerged from the timber. He shifted his anxious gaze from the drained face of the woman to the impassive features of Edge. Then nodded, reached a tentative hand for the reins, another to grip the brake lever. Plainly would have preferred it if his tacit request for permission to leave had drawn a response, but managed to squeeze out the request around the lump in his throat:

'So it's okay to leave?'

'No sweat,' Edge answered.

Ruby Red said nothing nor did anything.

Grogan let off the brake but did not flick the reins over the backs of the horses as they took the weight of the wagon that wanted to roll back down the gentle slope, asked:

'What about an address for the reward? If the company feels——'

'You know the name,' Edge interrupted. 'Could be I can be reached care of Adam Steele, ranch called the Trail's End, town of Providence, California.'

'Ma'am?' Grogan asked of the woman who had allowed her head to sink forward again, hair swinging across her face.

She said without looking up: 'Send the whole bundle to where he says. Maybe he'll see to it I get a share.'

'Okay,' Grogan acknowledged, and gave a sharp-voiced command to the team as he flicked the reins.

The rig moved forward, its driver looking neither to left nor right, his attitude seeming almost painfully stiff as he crouched on the seat, concentrated on not submitting to an impulse to order a frantic gallop up the slope and out of the valley.

Edge remained astride his mount, smoking the cigarette, switching his attention unhurriedly between the departing wagon and the hunkered-down woman, until the rig went out of sight over the brow of the hill beside the outcrop.

This took perhaps three minutes, during which time Ruby Red never moved or made a sound. But she was not so detached from her surroundings that she failed to hear Edge ask:

'You trust me, lady?'

'Like hell I do, mister. I don't ever trust any man unless I know him real well. Most times not even then.' Maybe there was a moment when blazing fires lit up her eyes in her downcast face, but her voice hardened just a little.

'So?'

'So what?'

'The reward, lady.'

'What friggin' reward?' Now there was just a hint of scorn in her voice. 'I'd bet a buck to a penny that lumber company's run by men. So I'm not countin' on anybody to take the trouble to send any reward anyplace. Once they get their payroll safe and sound. And you and me are long gone.'

'You could be right,' Edge allowed evenly, shrugged.

Now she brought up her head, rose wearily to her feet and showed her face was expressionless, like she was too tired to feel anything about anything. She left the Winchester on the ground with the other rifles and the revolver so she could use both hands to clutch the torn shirt across the front of her body. Said dully:

'Let me tell you, mister, where men are concerned, I'm right more times than I'm wrong about them. And I ain't gonna make no exceptions for present company. Most of them are bastards. Them that ain't are sonsofbitches. A lot of the rest are assholes. Nine outta ten of the others are creeps. And maybe one in a million of all them that are left might be the kinda guy I could maybe get to like.'

Edge told her: 'I ain't about to defend any part of the human race, lady.'

She shrugged, showed something close to a cynical smile. 'I'm one sour piece of ass, ain't I, mister?'

'I guess you got good reason to think the way you do.'

Now the cynical smile developed into a short laugh of contempt. 'If you got a year to spare, I could maybe tell you about it.'

Edge shook his head. 'I don't go for that stuff about a trouble shared being a trouble halved.'

'I wouldn't expect you to. If it matters a damn, neither do I. Was once told that keepin' stuff to myself is what makes me the mean-tempered bitch that I am.'

'You know where to stop by if you figure there happens to be a reward?'

'I heard.'

'If I've moved on, I'll leave your part of it there.'

She pulled a face, told him: 'I reckon if I'm in line for any kinda reward, it'll be the kind I'll get in heaven. Best to you, mister.'

Edge tipped his hat, showed her a brief smile as he replied: 'Guess the best I can wish you is to be good and die young.'

6

It was a firmly entrenched quirk of Edge's that unless there was a risk of being attacked from behind, he didn't like to look back at the place he was leaving.

But because he was in process of changing his ways, hoped to become a different kind of character with a new set of characteristics, this early morning he turned in the saddle of the slow-moving horse to see if the half-breed woman who had made such an impression on him was maybe peering longingly after him.

But Ruby Red seemed to be in a world of her own again. Certainly was ignoring him as he departed: obviously unconcerned if he chose to see her as a gruesome scavenger in the bright, warm sunlight of the newly dawned day while she robbed the bodies.

But his first thought was that the sun was not as yet high and hot enough, nor had the three men been dead for long enough, for the corpses to emanate the sickly sweet odour of decomposition. So if Ruby Red's sense of satisfaction at what she was doing was countered by a less welcome feeling about what occupied her, it was probably only a natural aversion to touching the remains of recently living men.

Then he tossed away his cigarette, spat forcefully to the side as he faced front and vented a low oath, irritated with himself again.

This time it riled him that he had sought to impose on the woman an emotion he could have no idea she experienced. And as he rode on to the tunnel-like strip of trail which curved through a canopy of trees beside the new born stream, his angry mind was filled with an image of what he had seen. From a distance that made it impossible to discern an expression on the woman's face that might even suggest what she felt.

She was down on her knees, once more unworried that her torn shirt gaped open to bare her breasts, as she used both hands to search through the clothing of the men. Looking for money or anything else of value that Harper, Singer and Wyler had been carrying when they died so violently.

Which was fine, Edge rationalised as, out of sight of Ruby Red, he reined in his mount, dismounted and led the animal to the side of the stream so both he and the horse could drink the cold, clear, good-tasting water.

She had been used and abused by these men. And although she had certainly gotten some kind of satisfaction from backshooting Singer, finishing off the gut-shot Wyler and blasting a bullet into that area of Harper's body that was the part of men she had been misused by so often, she needed something more.

Maybe she had taken mere revenge against the male sex in the past, and knew that its sweet taste was not something that could be savoured for very long. Sure, it tasted fine for a short time. As good as the water he was drinking, Edge knew from experience. But sometimes it could leave a sour taste in the mouth. And even if it did not, it certainly was no substitute for the more satisfying flavour of solid food when a man—or a woman—was hungry. And mostly the easiest, often the only, way to get food was to buy it with hard cash.

Dead men had no use for food, or the money to buy it. So it made good sense for Ruby Red to take advantage of the opportunity presented to her. Especially it was acceptable since the corpses she robbed were those of men she had good cause to have hated.

After he and his horse had drunk their fill, Edge spent more time beside the bank of the clear-running stream, using the water to wash up and shave. And as he did this he tried to think of occasions when he had found it necessary to rob the dead. But none came easily to mind and he rationalised that this was understandable. Since he had started to become a different kind of man, to whom such a practice was repugnant. And in the future there would be no circumstance when such an act would be necessary, either! Maybe . . .

After he mounted up, he cast a final look back with the specific purpose of chancing to see the blonde-haired, slender-bodied half-Indian woman with a face that lacked beauty but possessed so much more that attracted him. But she remained out of sight beyond the curving tunnel of trees.

Then, as he rode south along the valley floor, he surveyed the terrain behind him for the same purpose as when he glanced ahead or to left and right. Was the man he always had been and doubtless always would be in this respect: looking for a first sign that all was not well. In this instance, somebody or a bunch of men might be waiting in ambush. To stop him before he had a chance to enjoy the peaceful pleasures of a settled life he had only tasted in his formative years in Iowa and briefly while he was married to Beth, on the farm up in the Dakotas . . .

He made a conscious effort to blot those parts of his life out of his mind, told himself that, if nothing else, he had learned from living on the harsher side of the life's street that it was not possible to re-establish what had been good once it was lost.

Much later in the day, when the cigarette he had freshly rolled and lit tasted like dust soaked in coal oil, he reached the conclusion that maybe it was also not possible to re-experience the worst of times. But then, who the hell would want to?

The foul taste of the cigarette jerked him out of the reverie that he saw had held him for many hours. For the sun had arced beyond its midday peak while he failed to mark the passing of the hours. Failed, also, to be aware of the kind of terrain he was riding, in which it was possible for menace to lurk malevolently, become a dangerous threat, a lethal reality.

But he suddenly grinned at this thought. Nothing *had* happened to him. It was crazy to be riled that he had not remained alert to non-existent dangers. Ordinary men, of which he intended to become one, did not spend every waking hour concerning themselves with what might happen.

He did not feel hungry from having no breakfast and missing a noon meal break. But the heat of the spring day had worked up a thirst. His horse needed water, too, he saw as they both dipped their faces into the stream which was much wider here, several miles down the valley from where they had started out early this morning, leaving death and degradation behind.

While the horse cropped on the lush, new season's grass close to the bank of the stream, Edge dug out the makings. Saw with an irritated grunt how depleted his stock of tobacco had become. Recalled how bad the last cigarette had tasted and realised he must have smoked one after another as he rode down this Oregon Valley toward his destination in California. Unaware of and unconcerned with his surroundings, his mind filled with a mixture of memories of what once had been and hopes of what could be.

Then he remounted and pressed on southwards in the same way. Later saw he was no longer in the valley and suddenly found himself ravenously hungry while the sun was still some distance above the south western horizon. Thought it was probably not much past five o'clock when he called a halt, attended to his horse and gathered the makings of a fire. Lit the kindling, prepared a beef and bean stew and set the skillet on the flames, along with a coffee pot.

The valley, he saw, had petered away to a thickly-timbered plateau when the ground slowly sloped up and the flanking hills got lower. He had seen no marker and there was no dramatic change of scenery—neither of which meant much—but he had a hunch that he had crossed the state line into California. Which was no big deal, he reflected as he drank his first cup of coffee of the day.

The coffee tasted fine, and so did the cigarette he rolled and smoked. He had been to California before. Like he had gone without coffee for a whole day and smoked too many cigarettes before. He had also covered a lot of miles without a clear memory of the kind of country over which he wore down horseshoes.

And he had been hung up on a woman more than once before, damnit!

He pushed all these notions out of his mind: directed his thinking to just why it felt so good to be in California. Which was easy to understand. For this time he was not just drifting:

he was heading for somewhere special. Hell, he had even given Ray Grogan the address of Steele's ranch. He couldn't recall the last time when he had gone anyplace and known where he would be at the end of the trail he was riding.

Now he had this end in view, more clearly defined than ever because it was where the McAllister Lumber Company would send some money—maybe—he felt good as he bedded down. While the sun was not even touching the horizon, the taste of hot food was still in his mouth and there was enough of it in his belly to satisfy his need. Which promised a long night of restful sleep and an early waking, when he would be good and ready to push on to where he intended to get.

But right off this plan started to go wrong. For he had only just stretched out under his blankets, curled a hand loosely around the frame of the Winchester as he tipped his hat off his head on to his face, when he heard the clop of many hooves on the trail that ran past the place where he had made night camp.

This was in a small hollow halfway up the higher side of a shallow depression which probably filled with rainwater in winter but was dry now and provided his gelding with plenty of lush grass at the bottom. The natural crater was sparsely strewn with boulders and fringed thickly with timber, except on the far side from where he had lit the fire and unfurled his bedroll. Here, some two hundred and fifty feet from where he was bedded down, there was a break in the timber. The trail ran past this gap in the trees and it was from this point he had spotted the hollow within a hollow that made a good place to pitch camp.

Now he sat up, pushed the Stetson back on to his head and continued to grip the rifle as he looked across at the break in the timber. Not expecting trouble, but ready to counter it if he was wrong about the cause of the slow moving hooves.

There were at least three and maybe as many as five horses heading south, not being pushed hard nor hauling a wagon. Three, if he had guessed right about the situation: just one of them with a rider in the saddle.

And had the rider been right in making an educated guess about the reason for the smoke from his cooking fire, that had risen straight into the sky for so long?

The embers of the fire still smouldered.

'You picked yourself a fine place to bed down for the night, Mr Edge!' Ruby Red called, sounding a little tense, before she rode a horse into sight at the gap between the trees, where she halted it and the two others on lead lines behind her.

It was no surprise she knew who he was, Edge decided as he savoured the satisfaction of guessing right about her, along with a sense of relief at seeing her again. Probably, he thought, she had purposely started to make her approach clearly heard before she was far enough along the trail to look down into the hollow and recognise the bay gelding.

She was half Indian.

Which didn't have to mean she was skilled at tracking sign, he told himself irritably!

And she had drifted around the frontier for a long time, taking what she could get from the living and the dead when she could get it.

Which, damnit, did not have to signify she had acquired any special talents, either!

Even a greenhorn, who had not noted his was the only fresh sign that marked the trail, would have spotted the smoke of his campfire and known from the timing that the odds were short that it was Edge who had called a halt here.

'There are probably a whole lot more around, lady,' he answered tautly as he stood up, retained a one-handed grip on the rifle, barrel tipped toward the ground. 'But it looked good enough for me.'

He knew he felt tense because of the self anger with how he kept assuming qualities for the woman he could not know she possessed. Which was crazy.

'It looks real good to me?' she countered wearily and an inflection of her voice made a query out of a statement.

'No sweat,' he told her, and needed to make a conscious effort to keep pleasure out of his tone. Which was even crazier.

'I'm grateful. It's been a real hard day.'

She sounded totally sincere, this maybe emphasised to Edge's hearing because of the way he was having to fake his own tone of voice.

She turned her horse, lead the others down the sloping

ground from the trail. At the bottom of the hollow she halted
the animals near the bay gelding hobbled there and looked up
at Edge. Now struggled to inject a trace of lightness into her
voice when she said:

'And I'm grateful you didn't make any cracks about the day
bein' hard for you on account of you saw me half naked and
it... Lousy dirty jokes like that, the kind...'

She made to swing down off her mount, but she couldn't do
like the way she intended. She was a day more exhausted than
when he last saw her, and the minor effort needed to get down
from the horse was too much for her. The final dregs of her
strength drained out of her frame and she fainted while she was
astride the horse, collapsed back into the saddle, slid limply out
of it and landed hard on the ground.

All four horses were disturbed and sidled nervously away
from where she lay so still.

Edge made a calculated decision not to hurry down the slope
to the fainted woman. Told himself there was no cause to be
overly concerned about Ruby Red, who he hardly knew. And
from what he did know of her she was no kind of woman for
him now he was becoming a changed man.

So, after setting down his rifle, he moved slowly down to
where she lay and when he reached her he treated her in the
same way as anyone in need of help—with the ingenuous
gentleness that is so surprisingly a natural characteristic of
many big men, and in Edge's case seemed totally contrary to
the kind of man he was. But this was one of the ways he had
always been as he carefully picked her up and carried her to the
hollow, laid her down and covered her with his blankets.

Then he put more fuel on the dying fire, started a pot of fresh
coffee to brew. Checked she was still unconscious but
breathing easily, so probably had not done any serious damage
by taking the fall.

Next he went to attend to the three horses which were
already cropping at the grass in the bottom of the broad
hollow. Unsaddled them, released their lead lines and hobbled
them so they could move independently of each other within
the limits of their restraints.

He paid no particular attention to the gear he took off each horse, but saw that Ruby Red had slid a Winchester into the boot on each of the saddles before she confiscated the dead men's mounts and everything they carried.

He had already seen that she had appropriated the coat of one of the men to wear over her ripped shirt—the unfashionable suit jacket of Seymour Singer, whose height and build had been the closest match to her own.

He left the saddles and accoutrements in a pile near the contentedly cropping horses and returned to the small hollow in the side of the larger one. Where Ruby Red seemed not to have moved a muscle beneath the blankets since he left her. But she was breathing more regularly than before, like the unconsciousness of a faint had given way to natural sleep.

Perhaps she had awakened during the transition, but it didn't matter to him if she had. Unless she had recalled what happened to her, made the effort to see what he was doing and decided she could trust him. As much as she could ever bring herself to trust any man: and knowing that if he proved he was as much of a bastard as so many others, then he could do little to her that those others of his kind had not already done.

He sat down close to where she lay, listening to her breathing and watching the evening light fade into night beyond the flickering glow of the fire. As the coffee began to bubble in the pot, giving off the familiar smell he regarded as one of the most welcome aromas in his world.

And maybe Ruby Red shared his opinion, for as he poured coffee into his cup, intending to drink it himself, she uttered a low groan and her nostrils twitched like her subconscious was reacting to the smell.

A moment later her eyes snapped open, held an expression close to terror as she peered into the darkening sky for stretched seconds, remembering the worst of what had happened to her. But then those memories were suppressed by recollections of what took place later.

And she rolled her head to the side, to look at where the smell came from. Peered fixedly for a moment more into the fire. Finally looked at the man who she knew would be sitting

87

beside the fire, and now there was no trace of fear on her lean and angular face. Just a brand of dour resignation that seemed to imply she had no right to expect anything good.

Edge held out the cup of steaming coffee toward her and explained: 'If it hasn't all come back to you yet, Ruby Red, you took a dive out of the saddle. This will maybe make you feel a little more human.'

She nodded, pushed the blankets off her and shifted closer to him on her rump, heels digging into the ground. Then took the cup in both hands, brought up her knees and pressed her elbows to the sides of them like she was cold this warm spring evening beside the fire.

'I know it's a well-meant thought, mister,' she said dully. 'But I doubt I'll feel human again for one hell of a long time. I never killed anyone before.'

The cup did not burn her palms, but the coffee was too hot for her to drink right off. She started to take grateful sips: seemed to hold herself rigid to guard against the threat of trembling.

'You plan to stay the night?' he asked. 'Or you figure to move on when you feel a little more human, lady?'

She shot a sharp glance at him, like she was unsure whether she had identified his tone correctly. The impassive set of his features was no help and she started to growl:

'If you don't want company, mister, I'll be glad to——'

Edge raised his hand to stop her, said: 'Don't figure you'll be glad to do anything for awhile, Ruby Red. Except sleep. Just that if you plan to do that around here, I'll need to go bring a bedroll. They're my blankets you were under awhile ago.'

'Oh?' His distinctly hard tone still left her unsure about his true feelings. Then she shrugged and offered: 'I appreciate what you've done, Edge. If I could be sure of gettin' away from here right now without takin' another dive off my horse, I'd do it. But I don't know I could do that, so I'll take up your offer to stay. But I can take care of gettin' my stuff up here. Once I've rested awhile longer. Got some of this coffee inside me?'

He nodded. 'Okay. And I'd appreciate it if you don't make too much noise while you're bedding down. I'm planning a solid night's rest and an early start in the morning.'

He rose and went around where she was hunched up, to the heap of blankets she had left.

She watched him with a perplexed expression on her far less than beautiful but compellingly appealing face. Eyed him like he was some strange kind of animal she had never come across before—and she had been around a lot of animals. But when he met her curious gaze with one of his own, she glanced quickly away, concentrated on drinking the coffee a sip at a time. Stayed quiet until she heard him sigh as he once again stretched out beneath the blankets, the rifle under his right hand, Stetson shifted from the top of his head to cover his face. Then she said:

'You're a real strange person, Edge.'

'You're not the first to say so, lady,' he replied into the dark underside of his hat crown. 'But what other people think of me ain't something I care too much about.'

'Can I ask a favour of you?'

'Long as it doesn't mean I have to get up from under here again until morning.'

'Ruby Red is what men call me who ain't like you at all. On account of Ruby's my regular given name and my mother was an Arapaho. A Red Indian.'

'I know what an Arapaho is.'

'My father, who was married to my mother long enough before I was born, if it matters, was a soldier. A cavalry sergeant. He came here from Russia when he was just a small child and he had a name even I get in trouble tryin' to say. I'd like it better if you called me just plain Ruby, Mr Edge?'

'Sure, Ruby,' he agreed. 'I'll do that, if we got anything else to talk about.'

He had never been much of a lady's man, he reminded himself as he lay under his blankets, staring up into the fetid underside of his hat crown and hoping the woman would encourage further talk. The kind of talk that might lead ultimately to her making the first move to find out what it would be like to give her body to this man she found so strange, not at all like so many she had been with—been forced to go with.

89

But she said nothing more as he listened to the quiet sounds she made as she finished drinking the coffee, then moved off down the slope. And he listened harder then, grimacing under the hat, for sounds that she had changed her plans and was leaving the hollow: to ride for the rest of the night or until she found a place to make camp a long way from where a man—an example of a species she had good reason to despise—was feigning sleep.

But she came back up the slope a few minutes later, her footfalls dragging as wearily as when she went down. And she often sighed deeply and yawned her tiredness as she unfurled her bedroll and got ready to sleep.

Then there were some sounds that conjured up erotic images in Edge's troubled mind: fabric sliding over bare flesh as Ruby with the unprounceable second name took off her clothing a few feet away from him.

Next, without rancour or the slightest hint of censure, she said: 'I know you're not sleepin', Edge.'

'Nobody can do everything they want just when they want to do it,' he said, and only when the words were spoken did he recognise the unwitting double meaning they could hold. He pulled a hand out from under his blankets to raise the hat off his face, added: 'But I wasn't peeking until now.'

The embers of the fire still flickered with just a few small flames, and gave off enough light for him to see her clearly. She was kneeling on her blankets, facing away from him: so he had an unobstructed view of the ugly welts on her back. Stark black lines which stretched from one side to the other, covered her dark-hued skin at irregular intervals from the shoulders to the base of her spine. The scars of several whippings over a considerable period of time, for some of the marks had faded while others threw shadows off the firelight, still raised in bruises from more recent thrashings.

He was not aware he made any exclamation of surprise at what he saw. So maybe she sensed an almost palpable pressure emanated by his glittering eyes as he peered fixedly at her marked flesh, realised the level of pain she must have suffered from her beatings.

But whatever captured her attention, she wrenched her head around, managed to keep her torso turned away from him so he did not glimpse her breasts again now she had taken off Seymour Singer's coat and her torn shirt. She even crossed her arms in front of her body, hands hooked over her shoulders so that her breasts were partially covered on the blind side. There was a mixture of fear and quizzical surprise in her eyes, until he asked:

'Who did that to you, Ruby?'

She twisted her head still further, like she was trying to look down her own punished back. But she was not double-jointed and she pursed her lips in tacit acceptance of the scars and understanding of his inquiry. Stopped craning her neck around and carefully wriggled down beneath the blankets without exposing the front of her torso to him. Then explained:

'This was Vinny's doin', mister. Vincent Mitchell, you remember? Who got himself shot for cheatin' in the saloon yesterday?'

'I remember, and it was the day before yesterday,' Edge said as he rested his head back down, but did not cover his face with his hat against the present flickering light of the fire and future moonglow and starlight.

'That long ago?' she said dully, then sighed. 'And yet maybe it seems like a year even. Yeah, Vinny was one of the kinda men that like to beat up on women. Most times he couldn't . . . you know, get it up? He couldn't get any satisfaction from goin' with a woman unless he first beat her. At the start he liked to use his belt on my bare ass. But sometimes that meant I couldn't ride so good when we had to leave someplace fast. So mostly he got to pound me on the back.'

'Yet you stayed with the sadistic sonofabitch?'

She vented a sound of disgust, rasped: 'Mister, like I told you way back when, if you got a year to spare, I'll tell you about me and men. But that won't make me feel any better. And, like you said way back when, it'll only make you feel as lousy as me about it.'

'Did I say that?'

'Didn't you? Maybe you didn't. A lot of the time I mix up the men I've known, so it's sure as hell I'm gonna mix up which of them said what to me. But you told me you were tired, I sure remember that. And I'm real tired myself. So unless you got some kinda pressin' need I can help you with...?'

Edge's arousal that had started while he listened to her get ready to bed down had reached almost painful proportions when he heard the sounds of her undressing. It had subsided when he saw the scars of the old beatings on her back, but when she spoke so frankly of how she got to be so badly marked, he felt it start again, even though one part of his racing mind insisted he be ashamed of what he thought: for he had never been and never could become a man like that.

Knew, as he censured himself, that for as long as he talked with the woman, the harder it would be to ease the way he felt without taking her. Which would be taking her against her will, and if he forced himself upon her that way, he would be no better than Mitchell who beat her and the three men who enjoyed her body as nothing more than their due, because they owned her as a prize won in a poker game.

He struggled to put her out of his mind. Tried to recapture the pleasant state of impending sleep in which he had been luxuriously indulging, afloat on a sea of self-centred satisfaction, before he heard hooves on the trail. And was roused in more ways than one by the woman who had gotten to him so badly without trying.

But his mind refused to let go of the image of Ruby as he had seen her at her most desirable: sprawled on the trail at the head of the valley this morning, breasts exposed and skirt hiked up above her naked thighs.

'Something, lady?' To his own ears his voice sounded eagerly awake.

'What, mister?' Her voice was thickly on the brink of sleep.

'You said Mitchell was killed because he cheated. I watched his hand and it was a loser from start to finish.'

'So maybe this time he was just plain unlucky,' she allowed sleepily. 'I been bet instead of cash before. But I always got won back, along with the money put in the pot by the suckers Vinny played with. Most times, I was around when the game was goin' on. And I seen him cheat every way there is to get the best

92

hand. Hell, even when he knew he had a winnin' hand, he'd cheat to make it better, for the hell of it. Just like he beat up on his women to make screwin' them more fun for him, he never got a big enough thrill out of winnin' a game of cards unless he did some cheatin'.'

'Much obliged.'

'You don't have to be concerned about what happened in the saloon, mister,' she assured. 'Vinny Mitchell finally got what he had comin' to him, sooner or later. You can sleep easy, if that's all that's botherin' you.'

'Sure.'

'And if it ain't, then you help yourself to what you need,' she went on. And now she sounded indifferent rather than sleepy. 'But don't blame me if I go to sleep while ... And if you can hold out until mornin', I'll give you the time of your life. If that's what you want, mister?'

He knew she did not turn her head to look toward him, and he resolutely continued to peer up at the night sky, heard strain in his tone when he started to tell her: 'Lady, I——'

'Look, there's just you and me here,' she cut in on him. 'You don't have to pretend to be what you ain't and lie about it. I've known too many men. And even if I hadn't ... Well, I reckon there ain't many women who can't tell what a man's thinkin' when he looks at her.

'You want me, mister. You want me so bad it near enough hurts not to have me right here and now. What I'm askin' is for you to hold on to that feelin' for awhile. And you won't regret it, I promise.'

'Sure,' he said again, feeling a weak-willed fool.

'Tomorrow, we'll go on the mountain, mister. And there ain't many men I've been there with, I can tell you. The others I went with, all those other times, hell ... I can't even remember most of the bastards' names. About all they amount to is ... Shit, I don't know what they amount to.'

Edge growled caustically: 'A hill of has-beens?'

93

7

Even before he opened his eyes after the light of a new day turned the lids red, Edge knew he had been right to ascribe some of the best native skills of her Indian heritage to Ruby Red.

Ruby *Red*, that was how he named her as he awoke, knew she had left the night camp: in his head snarled the name she despised as he became irritably aware of the erection she had promised to relieve if he were patient.

And the double-crossing bitch had broken that promise! Used her Indian wiles to sneak off in the night! Moving with a silent stealth that had not interrupted his shallow level of sleep filled with dreams of naked, faceless women mixed in with idyllic big sky country vistas on which houses with bright paint and sparkling windows stood amid fields of crops waving to and fro in gentle summer breezes redolent with woodsmoke and cooking.

He kept his eyes squeezed tight shut for maybe ten seconds, forcing himself to consider the likelihood that the strong impression he was alone was nothing but a final remnant of his last dream: a cryptic warning at the moment of waking that he could not expect always to get everything he wanted out of his proposed new way of life. Be it a fine place to hang up his wanderlust: or the abused body of a woman of vast and mostly bad experience into which to expend the more primal kind of lust.

But he recognised this was much the same kind of false hope he held out last night when he refused to make the first move to take Ruby Red, waited for the woman to approach him. Like whistling for the moon, as his mother used to tell him and his kid brother long ago when they craved the impossible.

From a distance came the sounds of the creatures of the forest waking to the new dawn and going about their daily business of surviving until another nightfall. Along with the ever-present rippling of the broadened stream on the far side of the trail across the hollow. Then, from much closer, the even less obtrusive sounds of a single horse at the bottom of the hollow.

Ruby Red's horses, along with her flawed but almost painfully desirable body, were long gone. And once he accepted this his arousal diminished fast and he opened his eyes. Sat up and set the hat on his head. First glanced at the area of flattened grass where the woman had bedded down on the other side of the heap of cold ashes of the old fire.

Then he peered down at where his gelding stood, looking up at him. And thought at this distance the bay watched him with that brand of baleful censure which is an expression peculiar among animals to the eyes of a horse.

But he decided he was letting his imagination run away with him again: the gelding looked at him simply with the docile resignation with which most mounts regard most riders. Or maybe was trying to convey that it was time to be taken to the fresh water he could smell and hear not far off, so he could wash down the rich grass that had been supper and breakfast.

By the time Edge checked over his gear, saw Ruby Red had taken nothing from him except a little self-esteem by making a sucker out of him, he was able to come to his own terms about exactly what had happened.

This that, by force of circumstances or maybe even from choice—Ruby Red had spoken only in general terms about her past—she was no better than a whore, who elected to remain with any man who provided her with a meal ticket, no matter what kind of mean hearted bastard he was.

He was better off from having had nothing to do with that kind of woman. And now he realised this about her, and that she also set no store by any promises she made, he felt damn good that he had not sullied himself with her.

Which sure was a crazy way of thinking about Ruby Red

after all else that had filled his mind about her. And then, with a grin twisted almost into a sneer, he even decided he could think of Ruby Red as ugly: rather than as not pretty or lovely or beautiful or any other term she would certainly prefer to have applied to herself.

Just call me *plain* Ruby, she had asked. Or something to that effect. Well, if he ever ran into her again, then he'd do that: unless a whole bunch of more unflattering names came to mind first.

He knew he was being childish, but thought that could be a good sign. For after a man had lived his life one way for almost a half century, if could be it was necessary for him to go once more through his development stages if he were to become an entirely different kind of man.

He could not recall experiencing babyhood for a second time, but nobody ever remembered that period the first time around, so there was no comparison to be made. But he sure had felt like an awkward adolescent last night while he ached for the body of an available woman, could not bring himself to take her.

And it was surely another sign of the early years, the way he was thinking of her right now: cold-bloodedly taking her down off the pedestal upon which he had, for some reason, placed her. Undertaking an act of desecration out of a sense of embittered ill-will.

And, damnit, he had even recalled words of advice his mother had spoken when he and Jamie were boys!

All these unbidden thoughts raced through his mind, time and time again, while he broke camp, carried his gear down to the horse, saddled the animal, mounted up and rode out of the hollow.

Made him feel by turns angry, stupid and melancholy. Then, suddenly, he experienced a kind of anguish when he saw the area of ground where the trail went past the gap in the trees on the rim of the hollow.

The hard-packed dirt was powdered with a covering of dust that would have been disturbed by Edge's gelding passing over it, then the three horses of Ruby Red when she brought them down into the hollow and took them up out of it. But after she led her animals on to the trail while he was soundly asleep, dreaming wishful dreams, Ruby Red had paused and come back. Used a coat or a blanket to smoothe the dust, then with a stick or a gun muzzle or her finger had printed in large lettering: *Better this way.*

Edge did not like the feeling inspired by the simply-stated message. And with a deliberate decision to express hatred, knowing it was another childish act, he worked some saliva into his mouth. The spit tasted of the staleness of sleep and yesterday's cigarettes, maybe mixed in with the bitter flavour of regret. Then, with a grunt of satisfaction, he sent the stream of moisture at the words inscribed in the dust.

He touched the unspurred heels of his boots to the flanks of the horse and rode him to the bank of the slow-running river to drink. Did not dismount to take a drink himself before he turned his mount back on to the trail and headed southward, in the tracks left by Ruby Red's horse and the other animals she had stolen from the dead men.

After he had been riding for more than an hour, often able to glimpse the river, but seldom hearing it, a new sound was discernible. And he needed a few more seconds riding toward the source of the noise before he could identify it. A distant waterfall, or some rapids.

Even in the distance the sound of the fast-running water was somehow invigorating to his jaded mind. And when the trail and river came together, at a point where the water plunged among black rocks worn smooth by countless years of this eroding effect, he felt a compelling need to immerse himself in it.

He quickly dismounted, stripped naked and slid into the water just where its gently-flowing surface began to boil with white foam.

As its early morning cold took his breath away he could not prevent an exhilarated shout of sheer enjoyment from escaping his throat. And such a feeling immediately negated the unwanted thought that as well as cleansing his body, the icy water also acted to kill any last vestige of sexual arousal he might have felt.

He did not need to get out of the water to get what was

necessary to shave off his twenty four hours' growth of stubble. Drew the straight razor out of the pouch held at the nape of his neck by a leather thong strung with wooden beads, their once bright colours faded by time. He always kept the blade sharp, so no soap was required. And he had shaved often enough without a mirror to be able to scrape off his bristles blind, with deft skill. Did not touch the suggestion of a Mexican-style moustache which more than any other feature emphasised he had some Latin rather than Indian blood in his veins.

Since he had taken to wearing such a moustache, he was seldom mistaken for a half Indian.

Not that there was anything wrong with being a half Indian, he told himself as he climbed out of the start of the rapids, folded and returned to the pouch the razor that he sometimes had cause to use for a less mundane purpose than shaving.

In contrast to the cold water, the morning sun felt comfortably warm as he used his shirt to towel himself dry. Then he dressed until he was naked above the waist, left the shirt to dry on a rock while he rolled a cigarette and lit it, squatted and leaned back against the same rock. Enjoyed the taste of the cigarette, and relished for its own sake the simple pleasure of being alone, his own man with, for the moment anyway, all he needed out of life.

It was not often he had felt this way in the past, and whenever he did it was with a sense of foolishness, even discomfort. Like he consciously considered that a hard-nosed, mean-hearted, tough-talking, drifting saddletramp was not supposed to have finer feelings—especially over such an easily acquired form of contentment.

But now there was no feeling of being uncomfortable with a seldom-experienced emotion, as his face took on the lines of an impromptu smile. And he found himself whistling, albeit a tuneless melody, as he finished dressing, tossed the cigarette butt into the rapids and mounted up.

Later, he made breakfast on the move out of a hunk of jerked beef washed down with the sweet, fresh water taken from the rapids.

By noon he was as hungry as he was hot in the bright sun that hung in a cloudless sky. And he started to think about calling a halt, building a fire to cook up something substantial. Until he reached the top of a long slope and rounded an escarpment, saw smudges of smoke above a broad expanse of timber broken up by areas of pasture. He could even see, here and there, the houses with chimneys that gave off some of the smoke.

He figured that the scattering of places probably meant there was a town not too far off. Where he could maybe get a meal that would be better than he could make out of the ingredients in his saddlebags. And cooked better, by somebody whose business was to cook for paying customers.

Or, if there wasn't a town within easy riding distance, it could be that a family in one of the places would feel hospitably inclined toward him.

And if that didn't happen . . . ? And the nearest town was a long way off . . . ? What the hell? Then he'd be just that much hungrier when he finally got to cook up something for himself—too hungry to be over-critical of his own cooking. Today he felt too good to let his mood be soured by the kind of chow he was going to get to eat and where he was going to get to eat it.

The trail began to switch direction in long loops, so it passed the entrances of the farmsteads, instead of spurs cutting off out to the places.

The first two stone-built, single-storey houses he passed showed no signs of life outside of the smoke that spiralled out of their fieldstone chimneys: their doors and windows firmly closed despite the heat of the day. And because there was no urgency about fulfilling his needs, Edge felt disinclined to leave the trail and head up the tracks between fields planted with spring crops or in process of being readied for sowing with a summer crop. Ask if there was a town nearby, maybe get invited to stay awhile, share in the food already on the table.

At the third place by which the twisting trail curved, a man was working in a field. He was driving an ox which hauled a shiny new plough, watched by a woman who sat on an up-ended crate in the shade of a parasol at the house side of the field, a sleeping baby in her arms.

'Afternoon to you, mister!' the man greeted cheerfully when

he turned at the sound of a rider's approach, reined in the ox.

He was about twenty-five, with a fresh, heavily-freckled face, big teeth and large eyes that would make every smile a beam. Likewise, when he stopped smiling after he completed a double-take at Edge and decided he did not trust the stranger to be as friendly as himself, he looked almost morosely unhappy. And there was sudden anxiety in the way he shot a glance across the freshly ploughed half of the field at the woman who was about his own age.

She had much the same sandy-coloured hair as he did, but straight where his was curly. At a distance, she looked to be prettier than he was handsome as he advanced on the closed five-bar gate alongside which Edge reined in his horse.

They were both garbed in clothing of the same homespun fabric, dyed to a dark hue. She in a neck-to-ankle dress and he in shirt and pants, all the garments made with an eye to hard wear rather than style. He wore a uniform cap, the shine long gone off the bill. She had on a floppy-brimmed hat similar to the one Ruby Red wore.

She appeared vulnerable as she sat, suddenly rigid on the wooden crate, cradling the baby in her arms, gaze fixed upon the two men at the gate. He was tall and broad, powerful looking and, like the sight of his wife and baby reminded him he had something he would always be in danger of losing, he was now not at all anxious when he returned his attention to Edge. Instead, he conveyed an unforced confidence in his ability to protect what was his.

'Same to you, feller,' Edge responded evenly. He glanced toward the woman and tipped his hat, asked of the man: 'Tell me how far to the nearest town?'

The young farmer wiped sweat off his brow with a hairy forearm, then waved down the trail southward. 'Rikersville's about three miles, mister.' He clearly liked the innocent question and the tone of voice in which it was asked, tried another grin as he added: 'Less for a crow.'

'Place there a man can get a square meal, feller?'

'Tex Ford sells a lot of food cheap in the Lucky Seven Saloon, I hear. I ain't heard that it's real good, but then I ain't heard it's all that bad, either.'

'Much obliged,' Edge said and took up the reins.

But he did not order the horse to move forward, for the young man cleared his throat, said a little self-consciously:

'Martha don't never eat this time of day since the baby came. Just at suppertime. Scared of gettin' fat again, she says. And I'm eager to get this field done before I stop for grub. Otherwise, you'd have been welcome to come inside the house, share in whatever we was gonna have.'

'Appreciate the thought.'

The man on the other side of the gate hurried to expand his explanation. 'We just moved here, a couple of months ago. Wouldn't want it to get said around Rikersville the Shelbys ain't neighbourly and don't make well-meanin' strangers feel welcome at our place.'

'No sweat, Mr Shelby,' Edge assured the eager-to-be-liked young farmer.

Shelby jerked a thumb northward, scowled as he said: 'Like them folks live on the places you already rode by to get to us? Why, I bet the Briggs and the Stirlings, they didn't even trouble to pass the time of day with you?'

Martha Shelby called across the field in a tone of a loud whisper: 'Jonathon, you hush up talkin' about other folks that way, you hear.'

The new baby made a sound of coming awake, but was immediately quietened when the mother began to rock her arms gently and sing quietly.

Edge said: 'If the subject happens to come up while I'm in town, I won't have any cause to bad-mouth you and your wife.'

Shelby nodded, looking relieved. 'I thank you, mister. Martha, she figures that if a person can't think of anythin' good to say about somebody, then they shouldn't say nothin' about them.'

Edge showed a sardonic grin as he started the gelding forward, drawled: 'Maybe that's why I don't have too much to say for myself.'

8

From a distance Rikersville looked to be a large, sprawling and maybe bustling town. But as Edge rode closer, to where the broad main street ran arrow straight between the many narrower thoroughfares that snaked off at either side, he began to get the impression that all was not as it seemed at first.

The town was at the northern fringe of an expanse of rolling hill country that spread southward for as far as the eye could see into a light heat haze. To the north and east the horizons were provided by the higher, more rugged mountains. While to the far west was the Pacific Ocean, which disappeared from his sight as he came down out of the mountains.

Rikersville had looked big and bustling from far off because the combination of distance and the haze of the bright, early afternoon sunlight had concealed the fact that it was actually several communities merged into one.

Usually such towns, expanded and developed over many years, possess a certain attractive charm of the higgledy-piggledy kind: as different styles of architecture are mixed, when people of varying tastes build with contrasting materials to those who settled the town earlier.

But this pleasing effect can only be achieved if the new people who come to live in the town care about their surroundings: have an affectionate feeling for the place where they live and an altruistic desire to leave something worthwhile for those who come after. Be they their own children and children's children, or newcoming strangers who will continue the sympathetic process begun by their forerunners in the town.

But Rikersville had started out as a shanty town and had gradually gotten to be a larger version of the same: with no one section very much different from any other part.

A town where, Edge thought as he rode off the trail and on to the start of the main street, either only poor people lived, or the rich people chose not to invest any of their wealth in Rikersville.

Not the kind of town where he would want to live. And maybe, he was struck by the notion, nobody did live here anymore!

'Welcome stranger!' a girl of sixteen or so called brightly from the doorway of a derelict timber shack on the western, afternoon-shaded side of the street. One of a line of a dozen such shacks which all looked empty until he glimpsed movement and the girl stepped on to the doorless threshold.

'Obliged,' he said as he tipped his hat to her without reining in his horse.

Then he turned his head sharply to look at the other side of the start of the street. Here there were half a dozen timber buildings, more widely spaced.

The sound that had captured his attention was made by a mangy-looking hound as it ambled out of a doorway, sniffed the hot air, yawned, looked at Edge with total indifference and then cocked a leg, directed a yellow stream, at the rotted doorframe.

When Edge looked back at the girl, he saw her pretty face, somehow haggard for its years, wore a soured grin as she emerged from the shade of the doorway, angled toward him astride the moving horse and waved a hand in the direction of the dog.

'There are lots of us Rikersville folks would like to piss on this town, mister,' she growled. 'But then there are a lot of worse places to live, so I'm told. You want to tell me about some of the places you been, good and bad?'

Edge did a double-take at her as she fell in beside his slow-walking horse on the left, and confirmed his first impression that she was not much more than a child. But with the body of a woman starting to develop under the grey homespun dress that would have been shapeless were it not pasted by sweat to the prominent curves of her hips and breasts and rear.

Her face was smudged with dust and ingrained with dirt. And her hair was matted, long unwashed. But her big blue eyes were clear and bright and there was obviously youthful life and golden colour concealed by the dirt of her tangled hair. Her cheekbones were classically high, her lips had just the right degree of fullness and her teeth were brilliantly white: like they were the only aspect of her appearance she took trouble with.

'Why would I want to do that?' he asked her as he returned his attention to the hundred feet wide street.

It was now flanked by a mixture of one- and two-storey buildings: a few of them houses but mostly former stores or other commercial premises: some boarded up, others still with glass in the windows and doors on hinges, all of them abandoned. An occasional faded name of a store owner or a legend that told of the kind of business carried on at one time was still discernible.

'It's an interestin' town, with an interestin' history,' the girl answered. 'A lot of folks here wouldn't give you the time of day, let alone tell you anythin' interestin'. And most of them that would bother, they ain't so pretty as I am. No strings attached, mister? Unless you want there to be. You don't even have to buy me lunch or anythin'. Although I gotta admit, I could sorely use a bite. But I'm always hungry, which is on account of I'm a growin' girl, I guess?'

Her tone made it a query and suggested a *double entendre*, and then she stressed exactly what she meant by smoothing the palms her of her filthy hands down over her developing hips so the fabric of the dress more closely contoured the swells of her breasts for stretched seconds.

Edge still felt good, even though his exchange with Shelby, who was trying so hard to be liked in the community where he had just settled, had created a depressing image of the possible future, and he was now in this unprepossessing near ghost town with a child-woman who was acting like a whore.

He even felt a little reckless as he shifted forward in the saddle, drew his foot out of the left stirrup and extended a hand down to her.

The girl's grin expanded and broke out into a throaty, joyful laugh as she clasped his hand, hopped once to slide a foot into the empty stirrup and then was lifted smoothly up and into the saddle behind Edge without need for the horse to halt.

He glimpsed pale lengths of slender bare legs as she splayed them to sit astride the horse.

She assured him in an excited tone: 'Hey, you won't regret this, I promise you.'

She let him have the stirrup back and curled her arms around the front of him, interlocked her fingers. And then, whether on purpose or not, leaned hard against him so he felt the twin mounds of her firm young breasts pressing into the middle of his back.

'Do one thing for me, young lady?' he asked.

'My name's Gretchen.'

'Do one thing for me, Gretchen?'

'Sure. I will if I can.'

'Don't make me any promises.'

'Okay, if that's all you want.'

'Fine,' he said, and considered for a moment making the request that had come to mind first: that she should not thrust herself so close to him. But he had let too much time go by.

She read something into his silence, and said in a knowing tone: 'But it ain't all you want, I figure?'

'Tell me how to get to the Lucky Seven Saloon?' he asked, and discovered with a sense of relief he could live with the pleasing pressures of her breasts against his back without getting horny. For although it was certainly a pleasurable sensation, he figured the hunger for food was a more demanding need right then. Also, this morning's cleansing of his own body in the river rapids acted to make the stale smell of her flesh more pungent, which detracted from her appeal.

'It's right down at the other end of Main Street. On the left. You can't miss it on account of Mr Ford's place is the only saloon that's still open in this lousy town.'

'I was told I could get a square meal there.'

'You were told right. It's the only place in Rickersville where you can. Unless you're close with any of the folks that still live around here. Not includin' me, I should tell you, mister. I only

105

cook up stuff for Ma and me. On account of we're the only ones who'll eat the mush I cook.'

'Nobody's good at everything, uh? You're an expert on the history of this town, you said?'

'Oh, yeah!' she blurted eagerly, and took some time to organise her thoughts as they rode slowly down the right side of Rikersville's main street that at the north end was deserted again, now that Gretchen was riding with Edge and the mongrel had returned to the dilapidated shack that to him was probably a luxurious dog house.

There was also an absence of activity and noise on the mid-town stretch and out along the side streets. But there were signs of life, hardly of the bustling kind, toward the south side of town, which was sprawled across a slight down-slope.

'It got started when a guy called George Riker dug into a silver lode in them hills to the north,' the girl said at length. 'Up in the country you come across to get where you're at, mister. Mr what?'

'Edge.'

'I like to call my friends by their first names.'

'If we ever get to be friends, maybe I'll tell you what my first name used to be.'

'That time way back when you used to have friends, uh? I know the feelin'.'

'You're not so dumb as you try to make people think, are you Gretchen?'

'Sometimes I'm not anythin' people think I am.'

'You sure don't look like any kind of teacher. History or whatever. Or sound like one.'

'Yeah, okay,' she answered quickly, and he thought the words came out between lips briefly set in an irritable pout. 'Like I was tellin' you, this guy George Riker... A few years ago, I don't know exactly when except it was after the rush of forty nine down south? Anyway, he found silver in the hills and that started a rush in this part of the country. Course, in forty nine it was gold they found at the Sutter sawmill. Up around here was silver. And that didn't get so many people all fired up.'

They had ridden far enough down Main Street now for Edge

to be able to make out the sign on the roof of the Lucky Seven Saloon, a balconied, two-storey frame building that was the last one on the eastern side of the street.

Gretchen continued her account: 'But some men come runnin' when they heard what Riker found, and a few of them did okay out of it. Town got started, up where you and me met, and they named it after old George. Trouble was, though, there wasn't enough silver ore to keep many folks interested in livin' there for too long. But some of them that didn't make nothin' out of silver, they figured maybe the timber was worth stickin' around for. Didn't want to have nothin' to do with the silver people's part of town, so they built their places a little ways south.'

'The timber people didn't stay in Rikersville long either?' Edge asked absently as he saw that even on the south side of town, the side streets were lined by buildings that almost all looked to be abandoned and falling into dereliction: all those flanking this stretch of Main Street were commercial premises.

'Right. It turned out the timber business was only gonna get big up north in Oregon and such places like that. And when the timber went the same way as the silver, there was just farmin' left. Which you've seen there still is, up in the hills to the north. And the stores and the bank and the saloon and such that the farmin' folk need from time to time.'

'Yeah, I'm obliged for everything you've told me,' Edge said.

'And where we're comin' to now,' the girl went on like a well-practised guide, 'is that part of Rikersville where there's still some kinda life to be had, mister. If a man don't want to have himself a rip roarin' old time. In which case, he just has to ride right on through town. Head a few hundred miles south to Frisco. Which is where, one day, I'm gonna get a man to take me and we're——'

Now she started deliberately to press her breasts into his back, rub herself against him a little so her nipples swelled. At the same time, she made her interlocked hands into claws, dug the fingertips into his belly. But before he was able to speak the thought in his mind, which was to tell her he was not the man she hoped for, a woman with a world-weary voice instructed:

'Gretchen Erlander, you get down off that gentleman's horse this instant, you hear. I'm real sorry if Gretchen has been a trouble to you, sir. But you must understand, my little girl is not quite right in the head and——'

Edge had turned his head to the right, to look at the woman who gently rebuked the girl and fervidly apologised to him. But before he was able to gain anything but a fleeting impression of an elderly woman hunched in a rocking chair outside of a store, a man broke in, his tone of voice much harder:

'He looks to me like a man who understands most things real well, Mrs Erlander. Which I hope means he'll understand I ain't the kind of man who talks just to hear the sound of his own voice. Gretchen Erlander ain't what I reckon you think she is, mister.'

He was leaning against the doorframe of a building that shared the roofed sidewalk with several stores, two doors along from the one outside which the old woman sat, on the western side of the street. The window beside the doorway was similar in size to those of the stores, but it was glazed with frosted glass which had once been painted with gold blocked black lettering to spell out two words. Now just three letters of each word could be discerned, off-centre and at different levels: AL'S and ICE.

But the silver star in a circle pinned to the broad chest of the man who stepped out of the open doorway, hooked his thumbs inside his gunbelt and half turned toward Edge to ensure the badge was prominently displayed, left no doubt of what the missing letters had once spelled.

'I wouldn't claim most things, Marshal,' Edge answered as he appraised the lawman with the same kind of long and cold-eyed glaze with which he had been examined.

Saw a man five feet ten inches tall, broadly built with more excess weight than muscular development. Closer to sixty than fifty, with a lot of black hair, shot through with grey, a bushy moustache of the same mix and a sun-burnished, leather-textured complexion. His eyes were brown and had seen much of the darker side of life, and the line of his lips suggested he had come to terms with all he had seen, but would never get to understand the reason for much of it.

He was dressed in fine quality clothing, past its best but with plenty of wear left in it if need or personal preference demanded. A cream shirt, black pants, black spotted white kerchief, shiny boots with spurs and white Stetson hung halfway down his back by the neckcord. There was a far from new, unfancy Colt jutting from the hip holster on the right side of his gunbelt.

'Shit,' Gretchen Erlander said, softly but forcefully into Edge's ear. Then she released her grip on him, slid lithely off the horse and raised her voice to complain sourly: 'How old's a person gotta be in this lousy town to get treated like she ain't no little kid with a runny nose and no——'

'Gretchen, don't you start to talk dirty about the parts of a female body, you hear!' the marshal cut in. And the way he spoke, the way he looked at her—and she looked back at him and hurried toward the old woman in the rocker—indicated there had been occasions before when he had needed to take her to task: and she had learned from unpleasant experience to do as he told her.

'I wasn't gonna, Uncle Bernie,' she said, sounding like a contrite small child.

'I believe you, honey,' the old woman said, and held out her arms as if to offer comfort to a wrongly-scolded child. 'But you have to stop doing this to every strange man who comes into Rikersville, making up to them and——'

The girl suddenly whirled away from the woman in the rocking chair, quickened her pace and lunged through the open doorway beside the window filled with a display of pots and pans, pails and brushes. The door began to swing with a forceful shove. But by accident or design, Gretchen's snarled curse was clearly heard on the street just before the crash of the slammed door into the frame.

'Shit on all of you!'

'Please excuse my Gretchen, sir,' Mrs Erlander asked plaintively as she rose slowly from the rocker, her movements arthritic and her face contorted by a frown of pain. 'She's heard so much about the world but has led such a sheltered life herself. The poor child doesn't know how to act around grown up folks. She being the age she is and not having all her...'

She had picked up a cane she needed to walk, used a pointed finger of her free hand to make a circling motion beside her head.

'Ma'am,' Edge acknowledged, tipped his hat.

This drew a gentle smile from the grey-haired old lady who was at least sixty, with a heavily wrinkled face out of which bright blue eyes sparkled when she was not enduring the pain of stiffened joints. She wore blue denim dungarees that were a loose fit above the waist, tight from there down.

'It's good you understand,' she said, then moved to go into the hardware store, maybe to try to console the girl after her humiliation on the street.

'I'm real glad you took it so well, too, Mr...?'

The marshal looked and sounded as sincere as Mrs Erlander as he stepped to the front of the sidewalk, leaned a meaty shoulder against a roof support and took out a cheroot from a shirt pocket.

'Edge.'

'Brogan,' the lawman traded names. 'Bernard Brogan. We've had some problems with one or two passin'-through strangers and Gretchen. Lately that crazy kid has taken to spendin' most of her days lookin' out to the north. Hopin' to spot a rider. And when she does, she hares off up to the north end of the street. Feeds the man a line that's supposed to make him want to take her away from Rikersville.'

'Yeah, that's what I figured she was feeding me,' Edge said as he swung down from his saddle, his good and reckless feelings of a few minutes ago totally dissipated now.

'Trouble was, Clarice Erlander and her late husband had the girl much too late in life. Was touch and go whether the baby would make it through the first year of her life. In that time, somethin' must've happen in her brain, folks say. Hell of a thing. Mostly she lives in a world of her own. Tells a whole bundle of lies all the time.'

'She told me I could get a square meal over in the saloon,' Edge said, gestured toward the balconied building across the street. 'Same as a young farmer——'

110

'That you surely can,' Brogan confirmed, struck a match to light his cheroot, dropped it on the street and put out the flame as he stepped down off the sidewalk. 'I was just about to stroll across to Tex Ford's place and have myself a beer. You can get a bowl of beef stew any time of day off Tex. Not the best-cooked grub in California, I guess, but the quantity's sure value for money.'

'About what the farmer, a feller named Shelby, told me,' Edge answered as he and the lawman started across the street toward the Lucky Seven, that looked as ill cared for as all the other buildings on the south side of Rikersville. Like the business of supplying the needs of the local farming community had started to suffer the same fate as the silver-mining and lumber enterprises that had provided the earlier stages of the town's development.

As well as the marshal's office and the stores that stocked the basic essentials of daily life for people who did not want, could not afford or had no need of the luxuries of life, there was at this end of Main Street a livery stable across a wagon-wide alleyway from the saloon, a church, a schoolhouse, a bank, a stage line depot and a telegraph office.

'Yeah, Jonathon and Martha Shelby, I know them,' Brogan said, a little wistfully. 'A fine young couple. Have a newborn baby to take care of now. We're all hopin' they make a go of the old Henderson place. Maybe if they're seen to do that, more of their kind will come to settle in the Rikersville area. Young couples, startin' to raise families. Committed to stayin' around, havin' to stick it out come hell or high water because they got responsibilities. In place of the soured-up old-timers that never really did give it a go. Because they come out here to this neck of the woods to do somethin' else besides farmin'.'

They had crossed the hundred feet wide street, covering half as much distance again on a diagonal line. The marshal smoked his cheroot and waited patiently with a pensive frown on his face while Edge hitched the gelding to the rail out front of the Lucky Seven.

Up close, the saloon looked in a worse state of repair than some of the buildings that had been abandoned, its paint bubbled, curled or even completely peeled off the woodwork.

111

Many of its grimed windows were cracked, others were boarded over. The balcony that also provided the roof of the building wide porch looked rickety and several of its railings were missing.

Brogan saw the bleak-eyed way Edge surveyed the façade of the place and hurried to continue his catalogue of excuses for the town and its citizens.

'Tex Ford's been here too long, seen too many changes for the worse. One of the old-timers. Like Clarice Erlander, a lot of the others who run the stores. And the bank. The stage station and . . .'

The lawman hurled away the barely started cheroot, made no attempt to step on the still glowing end, scowled as he swept his gaze from the saloon and its neighbours to the line of buildings on the other side of the street. Then he stared balefully along its deserted length as he growled: 'Hell, what young folks are gonna come and take on those kinda businesses when the people that have need of them are dyin' out? Or uprootin' and movin' off some place else to see out their days?'

'Don't look at me, marshal,' Edge replied. 'I'm looking for a place, but this ain't it. And I ain't young.'

Brogan shrugged his wide shoulders, replaced the frown with weary grin as he asked: 'You allow me to buy you a beer? Or a shot of somethin' stronger? For lettin' me bend your ear about this town I used to think had a future?'

'Make it a point always to pay my own way,' Edge said, as his attention was drawn to the livery stable across the alley, when the doors opened and a black-bearded man emerged, leading a piebald and a chestnut gelding.

'Bernie,' the bearded man greeted, his expression and his tone dour.

'Stanley,' the lawman responded absently with a casual wave of a hand, then he growled at Edge: 'Hell, I can't argue with a man's right to do that, mister! But what about if I stand treat in return for the bigger favour you did? The way you didn't try to take advantage of that lame-brained Gretchen Erl——'

He realised he had lost the half-breed's attention. Saw Edge was peering after the man called Stanley who had turned to lead the two horses up the gentle slope of Main Street, northward.

'You know Stan Morrissy?' Brogan asked, a little irritably. 'He farms out by the Shelby place?'

'Not the man, feller,' Edge answered. 'But the horses look familiar.'

'What's that, mister?'

Brogan's tone had become suddenly sharp as he voiced the demand. And this switch drew Edge's intrigued gaze back to the lawman, whose fleshy face with the widely experienced eyes and faintly quizzical mouthline had lost all trace of its earlier friendliness.

'Something, Marshal?' Edge asked as he stepped up on to the saloon's stoop immediately outside the doors.

From here he was able to see in over the tops of the slatted batwings: and something he saw in the squalid, sunlit interior of the Lucky Seven made it difficult for him to return his narrow-eyed gaze to the lawman who came up on to the stoop beside him and countered grimly:

'There sure is somethin', mister! Them two horses were brought into this town by a breed woman. Claimed they were hers to sell, and sell them she did. To Pete Brinks, the liveryman here in Rikersville. Pete bought them in good faith and it looks like he didn't waste no time in resellin' them to Stan Morrissy. Now you tell me them horses could've been——'

'No sweat, Marshal,' Edge cut in evenly on the earnest toned lawman, and pushed open the batwings, raised his voice so the handful of people in the saloon—including Ruby Red—could hear him when he went on: 'Just that it was a surprise to see that feller with them. It was the breed woman had the horses when I last saw them. Those two and one other she was riding.'

He came to a halt, feigned mild surprise and then nodded curtly to Ruby Red who sat at a table in a far corner of the saloon with a man. Next he gestured with a hooked thumb as he went toward the centre of the bar counter that ran along the wall to the left. Spoke over his shoulder as Brogan entered the Lucky Seven:

'There's that very breed, Marshal. Long as it was her who sold the horses, and not somebody who stole them off her, everything's fine, I guess.'

'Well, I sure am glad to hear that,' Brogan said with relief as he trailed Edge across the saloon. Shot just a passing glance toward the table where the city-suited man of forty or so with a pale complexion and slicked down black hair sat with Ruby Red. His voice was friendly again and there was a smile back on his face as he exchanged nods of recognition with a group of four men playing cards, and three lone drinkers. Only he and Edge bellied up to the bar. 'I like to think that I'm a lawman first and last, but I sure do get irritated when business interferes with pleasure. Beer for me, Tex. And whatever this gentleman is havin'. He did me a favour.'

'I'll have a beer,' Edge told the bartender who had moved along the counter with a wall mirror in back of it. 'Pay for it myself.'

'Just so long as somebody pays,' Ford said as he began to draw the beers, his morose expression not altering by one line as he darted his gaze between the familiar face of Brogan and the fresh one of Edge.

He was more than fifty, short and broad, with a round, unshaven face and a totally bald head. He had the bloodshot eyes and purple nose of a man who had sampled too much of his stock in trade. He smelled like he had done a lot of sweating in his too tight shirt and crumpled pants since they were last laundered: his bad odour discernible amid the usual saloon stinks and the more appetizing fragrance of cooking meat.

'You eatin' here at the Lucky Seven today, Bernie?' Ford asked as he set down a glass of beer on the counter in front of each man.

Brogan looked at Edge with distaste, then at Ford with a stronger brand of the same expression. Shook his head and growled: 'Nah! Suddenly I don't have an appetite like usual, Tex.' He shrugged. 'Man does what he can, holds out the hand of welcome, acts friendly to a passin' stranger and it gets spit on. In a manner of speakin'. Reckon I'll just stick to doin' my job of keepin' the peace. Give up tryin' to save Rikersville from dyin' on its feet.'

He grasped the glass in front of him, tilted it to his mouth and drank the beer noisily without pausing for breath while he rooted around in a pants pocket. Then fished out a coin and dropped it on the countertop when he banged down the empty glass bedside it.

'Thanks again for not makin' trouble over the girl, mister,' he muttered with bad grace. 'Have yourself a good trip, wherever you're headed when you leave town.'

He spun on his heels and strode out of the saloon while Edge was still drinking the beer, relishing how its clear coolness washed the trail dust out of his throat. And, in the flaked and mottled mirror behind the bar, watched Ruby Red and her friend holding hands beneath their table as the other customers and Ford peered after the departing lawman with something akin to pity. Then, as the batwings flapped closed, the bartender returned his attention to Edge, picked up Brogan's nickel, said:

'There goes a big-hearted man who means real well, mister. Smart, too, most of the time. Except when he won't admit he's fightin' for a lost cause.'

Ruby Red was better placed to see Edge standing at the bar than was the man across the table from her. She suddenly sensed the half-breed's watching eyes and without her romantic friend being aware of it was able to exchange a glance with him.

At the moment their gazes met her dark eyes expressed gratitude, but an instant later a look of fear entered them: finally tacit pleading when she saw the ice in Edge's expression was not going to melt.

The dudishly dressed man with her, who had glowered ineffectually at Edge and Brogan when they first entered the saloon and spoke about Ruby Red as a breed, now recognised her dismay. And turned to look toward its source, would have gotten up angrily out of his chair if she had not rasped an entreaty at him.

Edge shifted his cold-eyed gaze to Ford. 'Lost cause, feller?'

The fat little bartender looked disgusted that Edge had not been paying attention, growled: 'Rikersville, mister. It ain't never gonna amount to anythin', but Bernie Brogan won't see it that way. Beats me how a man that's so smart in lotsa other ways can feel so strong about somethin' that ain't worth shit.'

Edge glanced again in the mirror and saw Ruby Red was leaning across the table, so nobody but her friend could hear what she was saying. He muttered, his own words hardly audible: 'That beats me, too.'

9

The beef stew didn't taste so bad as he had been led to believe it would. Or maybe it was terrible, but he chose to compare it with the last meal he had eaten in a saloon like this one—the bacon and beans in the Golden Eagle up at Ross. Instead of the fine breakfast Mrs Grogan had served him at the boarding house.

But, he figured, it was inevitable that he should recall the Golden Eagle Saloon while he sat, eating alone, in the Lucky Seven. They were similar in many respects, and especially they were alike because it was in the Golden Eagle he first saw Ruby Red: was affected by the woman in a way he would not have thought possible until it happened.

There saw her pass from one man to three others without protest. Here in the Lucky Seven he had watched her hold hands under the table like she was some fresh young girl, infatuated for the first time. With, damnit, a pasty-faced runt of a man. Who later had taken her up the creaking staircase at the back of the saloon, a guiding hand at her slender waist, as Edge carried his bowl of stew from the bar counter to the table where he now sat. And made time-consuming, inconsequential comparisons between saloons and the indifferent food they served as he tried not to imagine where the man was placing his hands on the woman in an upstairs room now.

Some of the earlier patrons had left the saloon and others drifted in while Edge ate the generously large bowl of overcooked but fine-tasting stew. He paid nobody any attention, other than cursory glances to check that they had no intention of having anything to do with him. And noted that mostly they looked back at him like he was the last person they

117

wanted to have any kind of dealings with.

Maybe, he decided idly once, this was because he was looking as mean as most of the thoughts that kept entering his head despite his conscious efforts to bar them. As mind pictures of the flabby, pale-skinned limbs of the dude intertwined with the lithe and burnished body of Ruby Red came and went and he could only replace them with other sexual images. Of Gretchen Erlander, little more than a child everybody said was not quite right in the head, but sure knew she had a good shape and had learned how to use it to stir a man's interest.

Whenever he thought of the young girl he felt a flush of shame at his lustful arousal, that he had been able to control when she was so close to him, since he was too hungry to care. And this brought a scowl to his face. Just as whenever the thought of Ruby Red and the man in the room upstairs replaced this and killed his lust instantly, a cold anger born of jealousy inspired another brand of the same expression that acted to alienate the other men in the saloon.

He also felt his features form into a tight-skinned, narrow-eyed, tight-lipped expression as he thought of what Marshal Brogan had said about a town like Rikersville needing new blood to bring new life to it. New blood, like that provided by Jonathon and Martha Shelby and their new baby.

Brogan's remark about the Erlanders having a child too late in life. A girl who was a part of the new generation of Rikersville citizens, but mentally retarded. But not too backward to recognise what a deadbeat town Rikersville was, and prepared to use the best shot she had to try to get out of it.

While the town marshal continued with the struggle on behalf of a lost cause: reduced to trying to interest the likes of a man called Edge in staying around. Not a young man, maybe even too old to produce children without running the risk they would not be born whole?

Particularly so, he reflected grimly, since he himself was maybe not in full possession of all his faculties? Because he was torn between lusting after the scarred body of an ugly half-breed woman and a girl with a simple mind who was still developing toward womanhood.

Was that now his prime aim in life? After he had made the considered decision to end his aimless wandering? To screw the kind of women that he would not have looked twice at in the old days?

'You don't like it, either?'

Edge looked up at the sound of the rasping voice, took a moment to recognise the morose-faced Tex Ford. Then dragged from his memory the gist of what the saloonkeeper had just said from the way the man's bloodshot eyes glowered at the empty bowl with the spoon angled across it.

'It was fine.'

'Empty bowl says so, mister. But some of them faces you pulled while you were eatin' the grub sure made it look like you weren't likin' what you were eatin'.'

'Bad thoughts, feller.'

Ford picked up the bowl, nodded sagely as he growled: 'Yeah, this town gets folks that way. Depresses them. But you're just passin' through. Think what it's like for them of us have to live here all the time?'

'Figure there are a lot of people think that same way, wherever they live.'

Ford nodded again, allowed: 'There ain't no heaven anywhere on earth, I reckon. But there are some places closer to hell than other places. Ask you a question?'

Edge dug out the makings, started to roll a cigarette as he responded: 'Should tell you I haven't come up with too many answers that make any sense to me.'

'The breed woman?'

'Ruby Red?'

'Whatever her name is. I don't know. Just knew she had the money to pay for what she wanted in here. After she sold some horses to Pete Brinks. So I sold her the stew and the beer. I ain't never been against nobody on account of colour or race or creed or whatever. A businessman in a deadbeat town like Rikersville, he can't afford to be a bigot. Or if he is, he has to bite on what he thinks. I don't have to do that.'

Edge said: 'I got no answers about prejudice.'

Ford shrugged his meaty shoulders, glanced toward the foot of the stairs up which the couple had gone about thirty minutes

119

ago. 'Nothin' so deep as that, mister. Sorry, I sometimes talk a lot of crap before I get to the point. Comes of bein' a saloonkeeper for so long, I guess. Listenin' to the customers talk so much without sayin' nothin'. Question is, I heard you tell the marshal you seen the breed woman before?'

'Couple of times.'

'She a whore? I mean, does she earn her livin' from peddlin' that fine lookin' ass of hers to——'

'She claims not,' Edge broke in and struck a match on the underside of the table, lit his cigarette. He tossed the dead match in the bowl Ford was holding.

'That mean you ain't sure?'

'It means she claims she's not a whore. And I ain't interested one way or the other.'

Edge was surprised at how easy it was to say: tell the lie without any tension sounding in his voice, experiencing any tightness inside. Maybe because it was not a lie, he wondered.

Ford sighed. 'Yeah, all right. But I got good reason for askin', mister. There used to be whores here at the Lucky Seven in the old days. When there was still a demand for them. They worked for themselves, you should understand. They weren't house girls. But the rooms I used to rent them, I got paid extra for them. And I just charged the breed woman the same as I would anyone else wants a room at the Lucky Seven. Same as it'll cost you if you wanna stay here. Same as I charged Mr and Mrs Fortune that are the only other guests of the Lucky Seven right now.'

'I figure if the breed woman took a feller up to her room . . .' Edge started to express the opinion, but cut himself short when he recognised he was going to score an irrelevant point against the woman through a third party.

'Uh?' Ford grunted.

'Forget it.' Edge shrugged. 'She claimed she wasn't a whore. I got no reason to think she lied.'

'Her room,' Ford pounced upon the terminology with an emphatic nod. 'That's what makes all the difference, I guess. But without creepin' around upstairs and listenin' at the keyholes, I got no way to know if that's where she took him, mister. If I knew for sure, I'd figure she's a whore right enough and charge her extra rent on account of what she took off Fortune. But if he took her to his room and——'

'Fortune of Mr and Mrs, feller?' Edge asked, faintly intrigued.

'Yeah. See, Mrs Fortune is visitin' with their married daughter out along the Pacific Road. Fortune stayed here. Had a bellyache, he said. But it sure got better fast after that breed woman give him the eye right back to the one he give her.'

Edge got up from the table, asked: 'How much I owe you, feller?'

'What?'

'For the beer and the chow? I'm starting to get an ache of my own.'

Tex Ford snapped defensively: 'Not from my grub you didn't, unless you bolted it down too fast and——'

'It's closer to my head than my belly,' Edge cut in. 'More likely caused by all these small-town problems I keep hearing about than anything I ate.'

'You're leavin'?' Ford asked, then lost interest in Edge, cocked his head as a horse snorted out front of the saloon.

'I'm leaving,' Edge confirmed as, along with Ford and the other customers, he looked toward the doorway. Saw a rider go by, having started the horse into a gallop from the next door livery stable, heading south.

'Hey, that looked like her, damnit!' Ford snapped, snatched a glance toward the foot of the stairway where he had seen Ruby Red go up, but not come down.

'And there's not more than one of that lady.' Edge countered sardonically, put two dollars on the table, his hat on his head and turned toward the doorway.

'Why's everyone in such an all-fire hurry all of a sudden?' This was slurred by a lone drinker who had been in the saloon since Edge entered.

Ford spat forcefully into the bowl he was holding, growled ruefully: 'I don't know about anybody else, Hank. But if I didn't have all I got tied up in this place, I'd sure be makin' fast tracks outta Rikersville.'

Edge pushed between the batwings, fanned a hand in front of his face as dust from under the pumping hooves of the galloping horse drifted up around him on the stoop. And he blinked his hooded eyes, trying more quickly to adjust to the dazzling sunlight after being in the dingy saloon for so long.

Apart from the racing horse, his own gelding hitched to the rail, and himself, the only other sign of life on this hot afternoon was Marshal Brogan, who emerged at the doorway of his office across the street, peered like Edge after the departing woman for a few moments, then called:

'That who I thought it was?'

'Ruby Red,' Edge confirmed as he stowed the just started cigarette in the same pocket as the makings, unhitched his horse and swung up into the saddle.

'What's her hurry?'

'I just know of her, not about her, Marshal,' Edge answered as he cast an impassive look northward along the broad main street of Rikersville. The town now more than ever like a ghost town, despite Brogan in full view at his office doorway and the low-voiced conversation that filtered out from the saloon, more discernible as the thudding of galloping hooves diminished in the distance. Like the lawman was a figment of imagination, the voices echoes of past exchanges.

Then Brogan drew deeply against his cheroot which he had smoked down to a final half inch, arced it out on to the street, said dully: 'Yeah, she's a woman, and who knows why they do most of what they do?'

He sent a faintly baleful look across the street at Edge, like he still resented him for not wanting to stay long in town. Then he swung around, went back into his office and slammed the door closed.

The buzz of talk in the saloon became the only sound in the hot air as the clatter of hooves faded entirely into the distant south when Ruby Red galloped out of sight into the fold between two hills.

Edge heeled his mount forward in the wake of the breed woman, but at a more leisurely pace. And as usual he did not look back at where he had been except as a part of the customary surveillance of his surroundings, to make sure he would not be surprised by anything unexpected.

Nothing changed in the town from his viewpoint for a long time. Except that the dilapidated and mostly abandoned buildings got smaller in perspective: and distance, combined with the softening effect of heat-haze, acted to mask the squalid grimness of the place.

At the same time, the grass started to look greener, the trees taller, the sky brighter, the hills gentler and the air to smell fresher with each yard he put between himself and the depressing, unprepossessing town he knew was not representative of Western communities. Was a long way from being the best: but also was nothing like the worst he had ever been in. So Rikersville should not have any bearing on the decision he made about whether he was going be a town or a country dweller in his new way of life.

Which was a sensible way to relate some of what had happened in the past to some of what could take place in the future. Anyway, there was no rush to make a decision. Smarter to think that at some time he would come across some place and know instinctively it was the one for him. Irrespective of what the community looked like, what kind of people were already settled there...

No, that was not sensible, damnit! Not smart at all. For with that thought rooted firmly in his mind, he could spend the rest of his days the same way he had wasted so many of the previous ones. Riding from one place to another down whichever trail happened to draw him. And he might never...

He had swung his head for what he expected to be his final glance back at Rikersville, before he rounded a curve in the trail that would take him out of sight of the town. But instead of sweeping his gaze over the distant huddle of buildings shimmering in the heat haze, then looking casually in other directions, he saw something that caused him to freeze in his attitude of looking back. And to rein his horse to a halt.

The southern end of Main Street was no longer deserted. A number of figures moved on it, dark against the lighter hue of the hard-packed dirt. Milling around with the frenetic haste of

123

people with a purpose. But not yet cohesively grouped together.

He was too far off to hear any sounds from the people of Rikersville who had found cause to suddenly spill out on to Main Street. But he could imagine raised voices as questions were asked and answers supplied, orders were given and acknowledged.

Then horses were brought out on to the street, and no sounds they made carried this far along the trail. But a single gunshot did—although why it was fired, which one of the figures fired it and in which direction, Edge had no way of knowing.

But the single report in the distance acted to set the seal on the hunch that had begun to form in his mind as soon as he saw the swelling crowd. A hunch that, whatever the reason the dying town had come so abruptly to life, it meant nothing good for him.

So the gunshot caused him to face front again, thud in his heels to demand a gallop from the gelding. And the horse responded at once with a will. Like he was also concerned by what he sensed was happening back along the trail ...

Which was crazy, Edge told himself with a scowl as he crouched low in the saddle, ignored what was behind him to concentrate his glittering-eyed gaze on the trail ahead and the country that flanked it. The animal was just eager for some vigorous exercise after the easy morning ride and the long period of inactivity hitched to the rail out front of the Lucky Seven Saloon.

It was also crazy, the way he had set the gelding galloping. Without pausing to consider the obvious: that it was surely Ruby Red's hurried departure from town which was the cause of the sudden excitement.

But it was too late for second thoughts now. And anyway, he was already linked with Ruby Red in the minds of certain Rikersville citizens. Had come into town not long after she did, admitted knowing her, left close behind her. Now had been seen to quicken his pace from an amble to a gallop when he realised what was happening behind him.

He maintained the high speed for a mile or so. By then the

124

gelding had worked up a sweat, but still felt strong, capable of keeping up this pace for several more miles. But mere speed for its own sake in this situation would achieve little. And could work against Edge if the circumstances changed: a horse capable of speed would be of greater use than a few extra yards of distance between the pursued and his pursuers. Pursuers whose own horses were surely being raced flat out over that first stretch of trail on which the gelding had been asked for no more than an easy walk.

Which, damnit, he would have concluded a lot earlier had his mind not been clouded by doubts about what he was doing. Whether in terms of the entire scheme of things, or just that he could have misjudged the events he had now elected to get caught up in by the reckless act of running from the people of Rikersville. Who maybe had been no more than vaguely suspicious about him until he started to run.

Now, a hell for leather chase would gain him nothing in the end. And whatever the rights and wrongs of his decision, with a hue and cry of this kind underway, it was better for the one man pursued to go to ground. Find a safe place to keep his head down until the initial impetus of the chase had died away.

He came around a curve and saw to the left a hillside strewn with boulders which had at one time formed a substantial outcrop of red rock on the crest of the slope: before some primeval electric storm or earthquake had crumbled the slab of sandstone and tumbled the pieces over a wide area. Formed the kind of ground across which a man could take his horse without leaving sign that any but the most expert of trackers could follow.

And it seemed unlikely that the disenchanted Marshal Brogan or any of his fellow small town citizens would be so skilled in such an art.

He rode his horse a few yards off the trail on to the slope, then dismounted and led the animal by the bridle toward the top. Heading for the crumbled remains of the former massive outcrop which were still embedded deep in the ground, jagged and leaning, many of the chunks of sandstone large enough to provide cover for a man and his mount: conceal them from riders passing on the trail below.

Sometimes he paused on the incline, interrupted his zig-zagging around the scattered boulders as he closed with the area at the crest of the hill that promised temporary sanctuary, to listen for sounds of pursuit. But always he heard just his own and the breathing of his horse.

Then, when he was almost at the end of the climb, he was struck by a notion that brought a scowl to his face, formed his lips into the shape of an obscenity: he had not even waited long enough within sight of Rikersville to be sure if what looked like a posse in the making was going to stream out of town along the south trail.

Something—he could not know what—could have happened to draw the group northward. Or to the east. Or the west. Maybe a telegraph message had been received. From the north or the south: the wire strung from pole to pole came into Rikersville from both directions.

Hell, he didn't even know it was a posse. The gun may have been fired in a fit of gleeful excitement and . . .

Who was he trying to kid, he asked himself as he felt the scowl slide off his face. First Ruby Red had hightailed it out of town and then——

Edge abruptly curtailed this line of thought and was impassive once more as he recognised what caused a short series of metallic clicks close by.

He froze to the spot just as he had been about to start forward again after the latest pause to listen for far off hoofbeats. But although his feet remained firmly on the ground, he turned his head. Looked away from the point on the trail where the pursuers would first show—if they ever did show on this side of town—toward the sound of a gun being cocked.

Saw the dark-eyed blonde with the plain face and the fine body step into the open from behind the rock where he had been headed. Eight feet away, pointing a Colt at him in a rock-steady grip, the muzzle trained on the centre of his chest.

The breed woman's expression was a mixture of fear and determination that Edge knew he should not ignore. For Ruby

126

Red was in the grip of unreasoning terror: the kind of powerful emotion that allowed for no coolly calculated thoughts about the past or the future as those times related to the present. She was aware only of the instant that existed: primed to react in whatever way first entered her head.

Her voice was as steady as her aim when she warned: 'I'll kill you, Edge.'

'I know you would, Ruby,' he answered evenly. Although his voice sounded a little thick with tension in his own ears. 'If I meant you any harm.'

'Don't you?'

'No.'

'I didn't kill that man, Edge.'

The baldly spoken statement did not shake him so much as it would have done had he not already figured out she was the prime quarry of the Rikersville posse. It required little effort to remain controlled when he asked: 'Which man is that, Ruby?'

'You must know.' She sounded like she didn't care how he responded.

Which made him even more tense behind his impassive outer shell. For if she was unconcerned by what he knew or believed, it was likely she didn't care what happened to him. And in her present state of mind, that did not augur well for him.

'I don't, Ruby.'

'Grant Fortune. It wasn't me who killed him.'

Events since he looked back at Rikersville and saw the apathetic town abruptly come to frenetic life were suddenly fully explained. He tried not to think of himself as an accessory to murder, and its consequences, when he told the woman:

'I didn't know he was dead.'

She didn't seem to register the response. It was only important to her she get her innocence of murder established. At least by the spoken word, to whoever was there to listen.

'I stole his money. And his wife's jewellery. I admit it. They can afford to lose what I took. I only ever take from those who can afford to lose some of what they have. Nobody can afford to lose their lives. I didn't take his life.'

'Ruby?'

Ever since she first stepped out from in back of the rock she had kept her gaze fixed on the centre of his chest, right where the gun was aimed. And she continued to do so, her eyes with a glassy glint now. Did not hear Edge, nor the distant clattering of many hooves that signalled the Rikersville posse was drawing closer, the men convinced they were on the trail of a killer. And a killer's accomplice?

'Listen, Ruby——'

'You told them you'd come talk me into givin' myself——' she started to cut in on him.

And now she lifted her gaze, to look out from under the floppy brim of her battered Stetson to stare into his face. With terror and determination again. But then her eyes widened suddenly, like she had reached an awesome decision: answered her own half-asked question with a response that was not good for Edge.

Her gun hand wavered when she heard the approaching hoofbeats and snapped her head to the side. And at that instant Edge made a decision of his own: fast but not panicked. Reached a conclusion that if he did not make a move to prevent it, Ruby Red was about to blast a bullet into his chest.

He dropped his hand away from the bridle, lunged across the gap to her. Reached for her gunhand and grasped the Colt in such a way so he curled his little finger between the hammer and the firing pin. At the moment when she instinctively squeezed the trigger.

Her mouth gaped open to vented a shriek of anger, or terror, or despair. But whatever the emotion, it was strong enough to constrict her throat, trap all sound inside her as Edge thrust his free hand forward, clamped it over her mouth.

The force of his momentum sent her staggering backwards, her head bent back: and she banged it against the rock with an audible crack despite the thickness of hat and hair between bone and sandstone.

He felt the rush of hot breath against his palm as she tried now to give vent to pain. Just as the revolver was surrendered into his grasp, her grip loosened by the pain.

They both went down. She into a helpless heap at the base of the rock. He able to balance on his haunches in front of her for a moment. Before he powered upright, whirled around toward his horse that had backed away in apprehension from the brief struggle.

He was aware that the woman was still gripped by high emotion. Liable to do anything within her power to strike back at the man who attacked her. Unconcerned in the present vengeful instant about the body of riders racing along the trail. But he had to ignore Ruby Red for stretched seconds. For the posse would surely have seen the hindquarters of the bay gelding up among the rocks had not Edge grasped the bridle again, hauled on it and snarled a command at the nervous animal to move into the cover of the rock behind which the breed woman's mount was already hidden.

Ruby Red stayed down and hidden, too. Appeared to be disorientated as she clasped both hands over her hatless head: clearly more to try to ease the pain than in the attitude of surrender she presented. While by turns she stared up at Edge or turned her head to look at the hillcrest from beyond which came the sound of clattering hooves as the Rikersville men rode headlong down the south trail, around the curve into the valley flanked on the east by the rock-littered slope.

Her mouth hung open, but she struggled successfully to contain a response to the hurt in her head, or fear, or hatred of Edge. And then she clamped her lips into a tight line, but needed to take a hand off her head and fasten it across her mouth, like she did not trust herself to stay silent without doing this.

But even at her loudest, a scream would not have sounded above the thudding of hooves that echoed and re-echoed between the slopes of the valley for a full half minute as the riders streamed past. A dozen of them, or thereabouts, Edge estimated after he chanced a quick look: judged the number by the level of noise, for they were already past his viewpoint as he looked down the slope and the dust they raised hung over them in a moving cloud.

As soon as he saw that nobody had broken from the bunch to angle off to the side, start up to where he and Ruby Red and their two horses were hidden, he returned his attention to the woman. His face was impassive and his mouth was as firmly closed as hers until the sound had diminished and he could speak without needing to raise his voice.

'Just so you'll know, lady. You ever aim a gun at me again, you better be ready to squeeze the trigger right off without talking about it.'

'What?' she blurted as she realised the sound of galloping horses was almost out of earshot and the fear seemed to drain suddenly out of her. And there came into her dark eyes a strange light that made Edge think the crack on her head had done more than stun her, inflicted serious damage.

'You see me clearly?'

'Sure I see you!' She was angry.

'You know who I am?'

'You're Edge!' she snapped, almost a sneer.

'Can you get up on your feet?'

She struggled to show him she could. He did not help her and although she did not yet trust herself to step away from the support of the rock, she felt confident enough to claim: 'I'm all right.' Then, with the sneering tone again, she added: 'Like I told you once, I'm used to gettin' roughed up by men and so——'

'This time you brought it on yourself, Ruby,' he reminded.

'But I thought——' she started to counter defiantly.

He broke in flatly: 'You got that other thought fixed in your mind? About never pointing a gun at me again unless you plan to kill me?'

She made an impatient gesture with the hand not pressed to the top of her head. 'Yeah, I remember. Way I remember you said the same thing, more or less, in the saloon back in Ross. I don't forget much that happens to me. Or is said to me. You scared me, mister. Way you came straight up the hill to where I was hidin' here. I figured you were doin' the trackin' for——'

'I'm doing what you're doing, lady.'

'You're on the run?' If she had been disorientated by the crack on the head, she was obviously now back in full possession of all her senses. Was convinced Edge told the truth, and intrigued by what he said.

'Right.'

'Why?'

'I don't know.'

Now she was scornful. 'You gotta know what you did that got them mad at you?'

'Right, lady,' he answered tautly. 'I know what I did. I don't know why I did it is what I'm saying.'

She was riled by his cryptic attitude, failed to read anything into the way he looked at her. She started to snarl: 'Did what, for f——'

'Got myself wanted for the same reason you are, lady.'

She glowered at him and shook her head, winced at the hurt this caused. 'You're not makin' any sense, Edge!'

He nodded. 'Seems to me, a man makes a fool of himself, he's excused making sense. Tell me about Fortune, Ruby.'

'How's that got anythin' to do with you, mister?' She could stand upright without the rock to lean on now, and she pulled herself up to her full height in a way that conveyed defiant determination. Then she suddenly had a notion that brought a scowl of vicious contempt to her face. 'Unless you're some kinda bounty huntin' sonofabitch?'

'Bounty hunting is a line of business I've been in. But not for a long time.'

She nodded her acceptance of this. Then her voice became as resolute as her stance and expression. 'What happened in Rikersville is my trouble, mister. I didn't ask you to butt in on it. I ran out on you last time and like I wrote in the message in the dirt, you're better off without me. I'm trouble, and I'm trouble for all the people I get tied up with.'

Edge needed to make a conscious effort not to reflect at length on how this was an opinion he used to hold about himself. He said flatly: 'But mostly you don't kill them?'

'The only men I ever killed were those three sonsofbitches that won me off Vinny Mitchell.' She sounded convinced she was responsible for all three men dying. 'I had good reason. Like I'd have had good reason to kill you if you really did mean to turn me in. But I didn't have no cause to stick a knife into Grant Fortune.'

Edge suggested evenly: 'So let's go back to Rikersville. Put that on the record, Ruby.'

'What?' The single word was almost an incoherent shriek.

'Way things have turned out, for whatever reason, your trouble is mine now. And I got cause not to have a killing hanging over me from now on. So best we go back to town, see if we can——'

She snarled something in a foreign language. Probably Arapaho, certainly an obscenity.

He went on: 'But you better talk plain American. So people there can understand what you're saying.'

She snarled: 'In plain American, mister, you can stick that idea way up where the sun don't ever shine! I'm a breed woman they figure robbed and killed a white eyes. And I ain't about to hand myself over to...'

He had been holding her gun in a loose grip down at his side ever since the posse raced by. Now he slowly raised his hand, pointed the Colt at arm's length so the muzzle came within six inches of the bridge of her nose.

Her composure was shaken for just a moment or so, before she showed a cynical smile, challenged: 'So you kill me, and then what, Edge? Where does that leave you?'

'Back in the bounty hunting business,' he replied evenly. And saw fear return to her dark eyes as she realised he was not making an idle threat. 'If Mrs Fortune has posted a reward for her husband's killer. If she hasn't, then I'll have to be content I'm not linked to any murder.'

'I told you,' she insisted, a catch in her voice. 'I never killed him.'

'And I believe you, Ruby. Alive, you can try to convince other people they should believe you.'

'And how do I know that's what you'll help me to do, mister? That you won't just turn me in and take the reward if there's one? What guarantee is there——'

He broke in: 'Guarantees only come with brand new merchandise, lady. Seems to me, we've both been pretty badly used.'

10

Once she realised she had to give her reluctant agreement to what Edge wanted to do, Ruby Red seemed to become lethargically dispirited: dejectedly resigned to meeting her fate, which had been transferred into his hands.

Or more likely, he thought as they got mounted, he pushed her gun under his belt at the belly and indicated she should ride ahead of him down the slope, she was merely facing up to the inevitable for now. Until the time came when she was in a better position to take control of the situation again.

Which he made sure was not right now as they picked their way carefully across the boulder-strewn slope, down to the trail. Then started back northward. He even abandoned his customary surveillance of his surroundings to maintain a constant watch on the woman.

On the level, unobstructed trail, he moved his horse up alongside her mount, asked: 'You want to tell me what happened with Fortune, Ruby?'

'I didn't kill him.'

'You already said so a time or two. What happened from when you were holding hands under the table and the time you started your horse running from the livery stable?'

She continued to stare directly ahead for several seconds, her profile set in a hard frown, as if to tacitly emphasise she was finished talking with him. Then a long sigh trickled out of her mouth and she said wearily:

'I'm not what you think I am. What most men think I am. There's a ... a purpose to everythin' I do, mister. It doesn't matter to you what that purpose is, but it's the most important thing in the world to me.'

She shrugged, seemed to be lost for a form of words with which to express herself clearly. Went on at length: 'And I'd like you to understand how a breed woman like me can want more out of life than I been gettin'. Driftin' around, gettin' passed from one man to another just so I can eat and have some clothes on my back?'

Edge had to drag his mind back to the present when she paused and he felt her gaze on him. Saw her Indian eyes simply asked for a response of some kind from him: did not express curiosity about why he had seemed to lose interest in what she was saying.

In fact, what she had said had acted to trigger thoughts about more parallels between them. And he clearly understood what she had said.

'You got it, Ruby,' he told her.

She nodded and peered ahead again, not with a faraway look in her eyes now. And she spoke in a mundane tone as she moved away from the background, began to speak of specifics.

'I did all right from my time with Vinny, and then those three bastards who won me off him. I mean all right in the money I got off them. And the goods I was able to sell. All I figured to do in Rikersville was rest up awhile. And get over the bad feelin' I had from killin' Harper and Wyler and Singer. That really was the first time I killed anybody. Come close to it a lot of times before, but never did do it until then.'

'I believe that, too, Ruby,' Edge assured her as he took out the part smoked cigarette from his shirt pocket, relit it.

She crooked a thumb and jerked it at the rock-strewn hillside that was going out of sight behind them as they rounded the curve of the trail. 'But I'd have shot you back there.'

'I knew it.'

'Like I knew you'd have shot me, mister. If I didn't come with you, do what you told me to?'

'One of the reasons I don't like to have a gun pointed at me.'

'Uh?'

'Main reason, guns can go off without people meaning for that to happen. Did for me once.'

'You got shot that way, by accident?'

'No. I shot my kid brother. Crippled Jamie for life.'

134

'That must've been awful.'

'Especially since his life didn't last too long. And being crippled that way didn't let him have too much fun. Another reason, somebody makes a threat, they have to be ready to carry it out. Or they shouldn't make it. And if they're not ready to carry it out, they shouldn't point a gun. But we're not supposed to be talking about what I think of anything.'

'Yeah, I got away from the point, didn't I? But there ain't no dark hidden reason why I did that, mister. I ain't ashamed of what I do, which is to make money the best way I know how to. To live now, and make myself a better life in the future.

'Like I stole money off Harper and Singer and Wyler after they had no more use for it. Took their horses, too. And everythin' on the horses. Come to Rikersville and sold the horses and other stuff to the liveryman there. Then, like I said, I planned to rest up awhile, try to get over the bad feelin' I was left with. You know?'

'I used to know,' he answered, and once again found himself drawing parallels between himself and the breed woman as he tried to think when he had last needed to pause and reflect with a guilty conscience on anything he had done. And all he could recall was how he behaved after the tragic manner of his wife's dying. Which was not a period of his life he wanted to remember.

'But it doesn't matter, uh?' the woman asked.

'Just to me, lady.'

'Yeah, it's nobody else's business. I think everyone should have somethin' private to them in their lives.'

'Like what you're working toward, Ruby?'

'Yeah, that's right.'

She nodded eagerly, and came close to smiling. But abandoned the embryo expression when he said:

'Fortune, Ruby?'

'Yeah, okay. Grant Fortune. Almost as soon as I walked into that saloon, I saw him lookin' at me the way a lot of men look at me. You included, mister.'

He did not look at her now because he had no wish to get into that area.

She went on: 'Anyway, I was eatin' and he was standin' at the

135

bar, havin' a drink and talkin' to the saloonkeeper. From what I overheard, the Fortunes were from somewhere down south in California. In town to visit with a daughter who lives a couple of miles out of Rikersville. They were stayin' in a room at the Lucky Seven because the house where the daughter and her husband lived isn't half built and there was nowhere for them to sleep. Fortune couldn't stand the sight of the husband, so he was takin' a couple of drinks. Help him face up to the meetin', he told the bartender. While his wife was upstairs, gettin' herself ready to go visit.'

She sighed, wiped a hand across her mouth. 'It was all borin' family stuff, Edge. But I started to get interested when he started to show the usual kinda interest in me, and he made sure I saw the size of his roll when he paid for the drinks he'd had. Then his wife came down from the room, all prettied up, with sparklin' rings on almost all her fingers. Like I said, I only take off people that can afford to lose what I take.'

She glanced expectantly at Edge, eager to have her basic premise for stealing accepted as valid.

He asked evenly: 'It was right about then Fortune got a sudden pain in the belly?'

She scowled briefly, then confirmed: 'That's right. He told her he didn't think he could make it out to their daughter's place today. Maybe he'd be okay to go visitin' tomorrow. They had a real loud quarrel about it. It was her did most of the yellin', about how he never had liked their new son-in-law. How that probably meant he was only makin' an excuse, so he wouldn't have to go see him. In the end, she went on her own. Like he knew she would, he told me later.'

'And Fortune started to show more interest in you, Ruby?'

'Almost before the sound of the buggy was gone from the street, he moved in on me. And because I'd seen he could afford to pay for his pleasures, I didn't do nothin' to discourage him, that's for sure.

'And he had his pleasures, mister. The poor sonofabitch ain't alive to back up what I'm tellin' you, but seein' as how you claim to believe everythin' else I've told you, you better believe I always give value for money that way. Better than any whore,

136

which is what I ain't never been.'

Edge was sure he did not utter a sound, nor alter the impassive set of his features. So Ruby Red must have sensed a notion that came unbidden into his mind. But she read it wrong when she hurried to qualify:

'I ain't no whore. I don't ever go lookin' for——'

'I believe you, lady.'

She stared at him, unconvinced, then reassessed her opinion of what was in his mind. This time got it right.

'I don't always keep a promise, I know. But if I take money, I always give what I'm bein' paid for. And Fortune handed over ten bucks, so I saw to it he got ten bucksworth of pleasure. The kinda pleasure that almost knocked the poor guy out. Along with the whiskey he'd drunk before we went up to the room, the time we had there left him good and ready for sleep. And that's just what he did right after: went to sleep. And if he didn't wake up before somebody stuck that knife in him, he sure went out of this vale of tears a happy and satisfied man in one way.'

'Not in your room?'

She shook her head. 'No. He wanted to, but I ain't no whore. I don't ever make my room a crib, so we——'

'And while he was asleep, you robbed him?'

'Right,' she answered immediately without any indication she was ashamed of what she had done. 'I took his entire roll. And the woman's jewels she didn't wear to go visit her daughter.'

She patted one of the saddlebags.

Edge tossed away his cigarette, asked: 'And made fast tracks out of the Lucky Seven and Rikersville?'

'You bet, mister. I knew if he didn't wake up of his own accord, he'd sure snap out of it fast when his wife came back and found out what happened. And I wanted to be long gone from there by then.'

'So how d'you know he was stabbed with a knife to kill him, Ruby?'

'What?' She snapped her head around to glare at him, her dark eyes aflame with anger.

'I said how——'

'I heard what you said! You're tryin' to catch me out, way you sprung it on me like that! I thought you said you believed me?'

'A lot of Rikersville people won't, lady. It's the kind of question they'll want to hear you answer. And you better answer all their questions with the truth.'

Her righteous rage took a few seconds to diminish. Then she nodded, sighed, allowed: 'Yeah, there'll be a lot of questions to answer, won't there? But all I can tell is the truth. And the truth about this is that I took a look in the Fortunes' room on my way outta the place. See, I climbed out the window of my room and went real quiet along the balcony.

'I had to pass the window of that room and I looked in. Almost scared the shit outta me when I saw the blood on the sheet that covered him. With a knife stickin' up out of the middle of all that blood.'

This time she used the back of a hand to wipe sweat beads off her forehead. The afternoon had grown hotter, but it was vividly remembered fear rather than the heat that raised the sweat from her pores. She had to swallow hard before she could go on: 'And that made me want to get out of town quicker than ever, I can tell you, mister. Which is what I did. Because I knew how I'd been seen goin' upstairs with him. And no matter what, everybody'd figure I did for him that way.'

'How long between when you left him asleep in the room and when you looked in through the window and saw he was dead, Ruby?' Edge asked as he caught a first glimpse of the south side of Rikersville emerging from the shimmering heat haze.

'I don't know.'

'That could be the truth, but it's an answer people won't like to hear, lady.'

She did a double-take along the trail, uttered a low, despairing grunt when she confirmed to herself that they were drawing close to the town where she was wanted for murder.

'A few minutes was all,' she said at length. 'I don't know how many. No more than five, I'd guess.'

'And you didn't hear anything from the Fortunes' room while you were clearing out of yours, Ruby?'

She shook her head. 'Mine was at the other end of the hallway from that one.'

'Nor see anybody who may have stabbed him while you were leaving?'

'There was nothing and nobody out on the street. For me to see, or them to see me when I climbed down off that balcony and snuck into the livery.

'Guess a whole bunch of people heard me ride outta town. But I never looked back. Just kept movin' fast until I knew I had to rest my horse or break him. Which is when I saw the rocky top hill. Went up there to rest the animal and hide for awhile. Was just gonna start out again when I saw you come down the trail and then cut off it. Come straight up to where I was waitin'. And I was sure you were trackin' me. Figured you had hired on as a deputy to find me, bring me in. Workin' for the Rikersville lawman who didn't strike me as bein' able to follow the nose on his face.'

'You shouldn't underestimate or overestimate people until you know them well, lady,' Edge said grimly. 'I made for the top of the hill for the same reason you did. Me and my horse needed to rest. And I don't figure Marshal Brogan for a fool. It has to look like an open and shut case to him, and if he's the kind of dumb cluck you take him for, you're dead.'

'But you're still goin' to turn me over to him?'

'Unless we find the killer. Turn him in instead.'

She snorted and pulled a face: a crude and unladylike gesture by this less than ladylike breed woman to whom he felt such an attraction. 'Fat chance of that happenin'.'

'Nothing worthwhile comes easy, Ruby.'

She looked like she was going to utter another contemptuous sound. But she sighed, then muttered: 'I sure as hell know that. More than most, seems to me. All I've ever had are the hard times. And right now it don't look like I'll ever get to have anythin' worthwhile outta havin' all of them.'

A silence settled between them and the only sounds on the empty trail this brightly sunlit afternoon were the slow-moving hooves of their horses. Until Edge made an impulsive decision, told her:

139

'Here.'

She had been peering fixedly at the buildings of Rikersville, now so clearly defined in the closing distance it was possible to see there was nobody moving on the broad width of Main Street.

She turned to look at him, and her eyes widened with surprise when she saw he had drawn her Colt out from under his belt, was extending it, butt first, toward her.

After a moment, she made to take it: then snatched her hand back and her eyes narrowed with suspicion.

'Why?' she asked thickly.

He nodded that he understood the reason for her mistrust. 'I'm no bounty hunter, Ruby. This ain't my town and Grant Fortune was nothing to me. I don't have the right or any duty to bring you in.'

She left a pause to lengthen to several seconds before she asked: 'Is that it?'

'Is that what?'

'I take my gun back and I'm free to go? You won't...' She seemed embarrassed and nervous as her voice trailed away.

'Won't what?'

'If I've got a gun, you'll have an excuse to——'

'Only if you aimed it at me, Ruby. You'll be free to go if that's what you want. But it'd be better if you head back into town of your own accord. Show the people there you can prove you didn't kill Fortune.'

'You figure they'll give me a chance to do that, mister?' Both her tone and her expression were incredulous, maybe her belief suspended in both Edge's judgement and the attitudes of Rikersville people.

'I don't know. But if they're not ready to do that, the gun'll give you a chance to make another run for it.'

'And you won't be one of them who comes after me?'

He showed her a sardonic smile. 'I told you before, I ain't a woman chaser, Ruby.'

He offered her the Colt again and now she took it. Glanced at it bleakly as it passed from his hand to hers. Then she unfastened the saddlebag which did not contain her ill-gotten

140

gains and dropped it inside. She did not refasten the strap of the bag.

'Why did you do that, Edge?' she asked earnestly.

'I told you, I don't have any right or duty——'

She shook her head, reminded him: 'At first it was because you didn't want to be wanted for havin' a hand in a killin', you said. But I don't think that was true. I think you care for me, Edge? Really care about what happens to me?'

'Maybe,' he allowed, and discovered he did not feel too awkward and foolish. So perhaps he had gotten over the second period of adolescence in his life.

She shook her head and looked unsure of herself and his qualified agreement with what she said. 'Yet I figured from the start you were the kind of man who just took what he wanted: when he wanted it.'

'Like I said, I'm not a chaser of women, Ruby.'

'What are you, Edge?'

He swept a cursory glance out over the flanking hills, for the moment experienced much the same degree of indifference when he looked again at the town. He asked: 'Do me a favour?'

'What?'

'If you figure it out—what I am—let me know?'

'Somethin' you sure are is strange,' she murmured.

'I've been told that before.'

'Way you just give me back the gun... Hell, mister, I could've blown your brains out before you had a chance to draw!'

'I don't think you're that good a shot.'

'Uh? I'm pretty damn——'

He cut in on her: 'To hit a target that small.'

11

As he and the breed woman rode closer to the southern end of Main Street, to Edge it looked a lot like when he approached Rikersville on the north trail a few hours ago.

But here there was no stray dog marking out his territory. And a much more desirable and available woman than Gretchen Erlander was on a horse beside him instead of riding in back of him, pressing her body wantonly against his.

Ruby ended a lengthy silence: 'At first, I thought this was the oddest town I ever was in. And now it's the scariest.'

Fear sent a shudder through her instead of oozing sweat like before.

Edge replied: 'That feeling could be why ghost towns are called what they are.'

'It looks as if the whole town went out with the posse. Or are them that didn't just watchin' us and waitin' until——'

'I don't know,' Edge cut in, as he continued to rake his narrow-eyed gaze up and down the lower end of the street. The left side, where the law office was among the line of stores, with a timber church beyond. Then the right, with the Lucky Seven Saloon, Brinks' Livery Stable, the bank, the telegraph office and the stage line depot.

He got no sense of being watched from inside any of these buildings, saw no sign of life within them.

'You're right, it is like a friggin' ghost——' Ruby started, and curtailed what she was saying as they both reined in their mounts out front of the saloon when they heard a sound, peered northward toward its source.

Moments later they saw a buckboard appear at the top of the slope where Main Street ran out of the midtown area of

Rikersville. It was moving slowly, with a single horse in the traces, three people up on the seat...

No, four, Edge corrected after he peered harder at the rig as the distance narrowed and he recognised who was aboard. The freckle-faced, sandy-haired Jonathon Shelby had the reins. His short and slender wife sat beside him and the youthfully statuesque Gretchen Erlander was on the other side of Martha Shelby.

The Shelby baby was cradled in the arms of the girl with the over-developed body and backward mind, who had probably been on the look out for a stranger to town, but decided the chance to hold a baby was too good to pass up and hitched a ride on the Shelby rig.

'Oh,' Ruby exclaimed softly, embarrassed to be perturbed by such a mundane occurrence.

'Out of town farmers,' Edge said. 'They probably don't know what's happened. Coming to town for supplies or whatever.'

Then he was as startled as Ruby Red when a bell in the short tower of the church shattered the peace of Rikersville. Then it sounded again, and again. And within moments its slow cadence signalled it was a death knell that was being rung.

Ruby swallowed hard, rasped: 'They sure don't waste any time plantin' their dead around here.'

The sudden sounding of the church bell had spooked the horse hauling the buckboard. And Shelby was having trouble calming the animal as it reared, was clearly near to bolting.

Then there was an explosion.

Which maybe did not sound so loud as it might have had not the funeral knell already broken the tranquillity of Rikersville so unexpectedly.

But the violent smashing of the window in the front wall of the bank between the livery stable and the telegraph office somehow sounded more ear-splittingly loud.

Myriad shards of broken glass sprayed across the street, and acrid black smoke billowed out of the blasted building.

Inside, a man vented a shrill yell of elation, and a woman trilled with excited laughter.

The horse drawing the buckboard was further unnerved by the explosion. And at the moment the animal caught a scent of smoke, he bolted. In such a degree of blind panic he galloped down the sloping street, toward the reeking aftermath of the blast.

'What in hell's happenin'?'

Ruby's voice was strained as, like Edge she stared from the hurtling rig to the bank: then across the street to where the doors in the arched entrance of the church had opened and a preacher had emerged, trailed by four pallbearers with a pine casket balanced on their shoulders.

'A whole lot, and none of it good,' Edge rasped.

Then he angled his horse to the side, thudded in his heels to spur him to the front of the Lucky Seven Saloon. Reined in the snorting gelding and drew the Winchester from the boot as he hurled himself out of the saddle.

Across the street, the head of the funeral cortège had abruptly halted in a frozen tableau at the doorway of the church. The bell ceased to toll. And from within the church came a chorus of demanding voices.

Along the street, Jonathon Shelby was losing his struggle to bring his horse under control.

Closer, Ruby Red suddenly had trouble with her mount which baulked at following in the wake of Edge's horse: refused to come closer to the scene of the explosion. Where there was no noise now, most of the smoke was gone but the stink of burnt powder still emanated from the sooted window frame.

Finally, the breed woman became angrily impatient, threw herself off the animal and snarled a stream of what was surely Arapaho obscenities. As she came clear of the horse, she dragged off the pair of saddlebags, one containing her loot, the other her gun. And sprinted to where Edge swung up on to the hitching rail, then hauled himself on to the rickety balcony. It groaned under his weight, but held.

'Here!' she yelled, and as he looked down at her she hurled the saddlebags up at him.

He caught them, made to lean down to give her a hand up on to the balcony. But with the smooth ease and lithe suppleness of the young and her Indian heritage, she seemed almost to float effortlessly up off the street, on to the rail, and then was beside him on the balcony without showing a trace of exertion.

'I ain't never needed a man to lend me a hand with that kinda stuff, mister,' she boasted proudly. 'What now?'

But he had already swung away from her, draped her saddlebags over the balcony rail, and started for the far end of the balcony, Winchester angled across the front of his body.

She rooted into one of her saddlebags for the Colt stowed there, yelled: 'Wait for me, Goddamnit!'

By now the coffin was on the ground out front of the church doorway, abandoned in panic by the pallbearers and the preacher when they saw the bank was being robbed, turned to force their way back inside the church against a concerted effort by the congregation inside to surge out: see for themselves what was happening.

Elsewhere, Ruby Red's spooked mount had turned and bolted out on the south trail, driven to do so by the way the horse in the buckboard traces was galloping headlong down the sloping street, ignoring Shelby's frantic efforts to bring him to a halt. While his wife, having reclaimed her baby, hugged it to her and also embraced Gretchen Erlander.

Then a man lunged out of the bank, a revolver clutched in each hand.

Behind him, a woman appeared, each of her hands fisted around the closed mouth of a gunny-sack.

He was tall and broad, garbed like a farmer in stained and patched work clothes. In his mid-twenties, he had dark and curly hair above a flushed face smudged with soot from the explosion. He swayed as he came to a halt after the dash from the bank, like a man unsteady on his feet from being drunk. Maybe he was drunk, on elation.

The woman, who held the two bulging gunny-sacks high and swung them like she was displaying hard-won trophies, was about the same age as the man. A redhead with a thick body and a face that would have been pretty were it not so fleshy. She wore a shirt and a bib apron, both garments tight-fitting on her lumpy body.

145

The sudden appearance of the couple caused a hurried withdrawal from the church doorway.

Then one of the bank robber's guns exploded a shot. And a woman screamed, her voice piercingly shrill: loud enough to ring out clearly above the thudding of galloping hooves, the clatter of spinning wheelrims as the buckboard raced over the final stretch of Main Street, an elongated cloud of dust streaming behind it.

Close enough for Edge up on the saloon balcony to see Martha Shelby's mouth was gaped wide, had vented the scream as she hugged her baby tight to her body. While her husband was also gripped by horror, laced with anger as he half rose from the seat, to apply every ounce of his powerful strength to hauling on the reins.

The body of Gretchen Erlander was held rigid as a crimson stain blossomed across the sweat-patched back of her dowdy dress. Before she was hurled off the bucking rig, thudded unfeelingly to the street, bounced, rolled and came to rest a dozen feet from the two bank robbers.

They had been about to whirl, duck into the alley between the bank and the livery stable. But now they froze for a stretched second, horror at what had happened etched deep into their faces. And the contrast of the elation they had felt only moments ago acted to make the expressions of this new emotion more pronounced. Before determination to escape the suddenly altered situation re-shaped their soot smudged features.

The buckboard raced beyond the bank, the livery and then the saloon. Hurtled out along the open trail, those aboard it safe if Shelby could hold the bolting horse to a straight line, keep him from making any sharp turn that would tip the rig over, send him and his wife and baby crashing to the ground.

The congregation at the interrupted funeral service were also safe, so long as they remained in the church. But one member did not do so.

It was the arthritic, grey-haired Clarice Erlander who emerged from the arched doorway, moved awkwardly without her cane out into the afternoon sunlight. Her deeply lined cheeks began to run with sparkling tears as she advanced

146

painfully toward the inert form of her daughter: born to her so late in life, taken from her so young.

'Clarice!' a man bellowed from within the church.

'Bess! Dan!'

This from a woman as she plunged out of the church behind Mrs Erlander. She was dressed in full mourning, including a veil that masked her face. Which perhaps impaired her vision as much as grief, for she failed to see the abandoned coffin. And she hit it with her leading foot, tumbled forward and sprawled across it with a shriek of pain or alarm or horror.

'Shit, I heard him use them names!' Ruby blurted. 'They're Bess and Dan Walker! That's the daughter and her husband down there!'

'Stay back!' Walker snarled. He swung both guns to cover the old woman who advanced unwaveringly across the street. 'It was an accident! The gun went off! I didn't mean to . . . But I'll . . .'

Clarice Erlander perhaps did not hear him. Or it was more likely she elected to ignore him as she continued to come forward at the same unvarying pace. But now she raised her arms, pushed them out in front of her. And the disease stiffened joints formed her hands into claws, while the pain of her arthritis and the effort needed to walk without a cane caused her face to take the shape of a scowling mask. Or maybe it was anguish for her dead daughter.

Dan Walker mistook it for hatred and was within a split second of firing both guns at Mrs Erlander when the woman in black struggled to her feet, shrieked:

'You can't do it, son!'

'You friggin' wanna bet!' he countered, pushed his arms out to full stretch.

Edge already had the Winchester stock at his shoulder. The hammer back. His finger curled to the trigger. He exploded a shot, murmured: 'Oh, shit!'

He was aware he was probably too late. But took no chance in the event he was not. So it was a head shot, that killed Dan Walker an instant after the bullet drilled though the back of his skull, rifled through his brain and blasted gorily clear of his face.

The force of impact at this short range slammed him down like a felled tree. And when his shocked nervous system spasmed a final garbled message to his hands, caused his trigger fingers to jerk, both guns were aimed down at the street.

'Dan!' his wife shrieked.

Her head snapped around to stare up at Edge, then she looked down again at the man sprawled on the street as both guns slipped from his open hands.

The gunshots ended the stretched seconds of anguish to the exclusion of all else that Clarice Erlander had been experiencing. And she became aware of her physical pain. So she cautiously lowered herself down on to her knees beside the dead Gretchen, winced and maybe uttered small sounds at the pain this caused her.

Mrs Fortune had come to a halt on the centre of the street, her arms stiffly down at her sides, the fists clenched tightly so her knuckles were white, her expression still concealed in back of the fine mesh veil.

Edge murmured a more forceful obscenity as he lowered the stock and canted the barrel of the rifle to his shoulder. Struggled to contain the mounting self anger that he had once again horned in on the troubles of a town that meant nothing to him: taken a hand in the destinies of people who were nothing to him.

With a single exception: maybe?

'It was you who said to come back here,' Ruby accused. 'If we hadn't, none of this would've been any of our——'

He turned to look at the breed woman and saw a strange expression on her plain face: a sympathetic understanding of how he felt with, in back of this, a tightly controlled anger with him for doing what he had done, and involving her in its violent ramifications.

She held his quizzical gaze for only a moment, then her eyes darted to the sides of their sockets. She had seen something on the periphery of her vision that abruptly displaced the odd expression with instantly recognisable panicked fear.

'Watch out!'

She lunged to the side, brought up her right arm to aim the Colt down over the balcony rail. Thumbed back the hammer and squeezed the trigger as Edge swept his gaze in the same direction to discover what had caused the sudden change in her.

The fleshy faced, lumpy bodied Bess Walker was down on her haunches beside her husband's corpse: half turned toward the saloon, her right hand raised to point one of the dead man's revolvers. Her mouth was wide as she tried to give vent to a scream, an accusation or a denial. But the depth of whatever emotion she felt was so powerful it constricted her vocal chords so she was unable to voice whatever was in her mind.

Ruby Red demonstrated it had been no idle boast when she claimed to be a fine shot. For the bullet that blasted from the Colt took Bess Walker in the centre of the chest. Forced a shriek of pain and despair out of the ready opened mouth. Then a death rattle as she sprawled out on her back.

A rumble of shocked voices sounded from the church doorway as the congregation which had started to come out was halted by the reports of the latest shots.

'She'd have shot you for killin' him, Edge,' Ruby Red explained. And saw something in his face that concentrated her gaze there: like her eyes were trapped there and she could not believe what she saw.

Edge didn't know, either. For although he had firm control of the turmoil of emotions that churned and silently screamed for supremacy deep inside him, he felt helplessly unable to form his features into their usual impassive set in such a situation. Just what the hell kind of feeling was he showing to the breed woman?

'That's the whore killed my husband!' the woman in deep mourning screamed.

Ruby Red dragged her intrigued gaze away from Edge's face as he whirled. A fusillade of gunshots blasted out.

Edge glimpsed the Fortune woman as she stood in much the same attitude as her son-in-law a few moments ago: a gun gripped in each hand. But she was firing blind, her eyes tightly squeezed closed, he saw before he reacted to the cracking of bullets around his head: dropped into a crouch as he pumped the action of the Winchester.

'I'm not a whore!' Ruby Red shrieked.

She brought up her hand, her attitude and expression and the way she thrust out the Colt warning of a compelling need to back the claim with violent action. 'Nobody calls me a whore and gets away with——'

Bullets from the two guns which bucked in the inexperienced hands of the grief-stricken woman on the street had blasted holes in the balcony floor and the saloon's façade, smashed a window. Now one hit the breed woman. And then another. Both drove deep into her body with a force of impact that slammed her across the balcony, bounced her off the wall of the saloon and brought her staggering forward.

She banged hard into the balcony rail and railings. With enough force to smash through the rotted timber. Her Colt clattered to the street along with lengths of broken timber.

Edge was starting to bring his Winchester to aim at the deranged woman below. Then heard both her guns rattle empty and realised that danger was past. Dropped the rifle and was in time to reach out and grasp the breed woman by both wrists as she tumbled off the balcony.

She was no light weight and he had to thud hard down on to his knees when her falling form jerked to a halt.

It was just one floor down, and with her arms and his at full stretch her feet dangled just a dozen or so inches off the ground in front of the Lucky Seven's building-wide porch. But it was important to him that he should haul her up on to the balcony rather than lower her down on to the street.

'I ain't a whore, Edge,' she forced out through gritted teeth.

'I know it,' he said, concentrating on her face which was full up toward him, her head hanging back between her raised arms like she had no strength in her neck. But he could not avoid seeing the blood-sodden front of her stolen jacket, getting wetter by the moment as the bullet wounds in her left breast continued to leak.

'I'm a thief. I don't keep the promises I make. And I kill people. But I ain't no whore.'

'You kill people, Ruby?' he rasped.

'Yeah, I'm a liar, too,' she admitted.

And something akin to a knowing smile spread across her

150

less than pretty, all-woman face as she died. Then her head bent back even further, which stretched and narrowed her windpipe. Trapped the death rattle in her throat until he let go of her wrists and she thudded to the ground, collapsed into an untidy heap, legs and arms askew.

Edge got to his feet, feeling empty. Which he recognised as being good, because if he had felt anything else right then, he was certain he would have been sick to his stomach as he looked from the dead breed woman to the dead Gretchen Erlander, then the dead Bess and Dan Walker.

Next saw that nobody on the street as the crowd from the church converged on the corpses and Mrs Erlander and Mrs Fortune paid any attention to him.

There was a slight sound behind him and Edge turned without haste to see Tex Ford stood at the bullet-shattered window. The saloonkeeper looked even more morose than usual as he swallowed hard, shifted his melancholy gaze from the street filled with death and late afternoon shadows, looked at Edge and squeezed out:

'I tell you, mister, this town has seen a whole lot of bad times. But this has gotta be the worst day ever, I reckon.'

Edge swallowed, too: an acid bile that threatened to trigger nausea. Then he muttered grimly: 'So Rikersville and me do share something in common.'

12

The posse headed up by Marshal Brogan had not returned to town by late evening. By which time Edge's throat felt raw from smoking too many cigarettes too fast, and he had a fuzzy head because of over indulgence in liquor.

He had abused his body this way as he sat in the Lucky Seven Saloon, at the same table as earlier this day that was maybe not the worst in his life. But it came pretty damn close.

At first he was the only person in the place: had helped himself to a fresh bottle of whiskey off the shelf behind the bar counter and started to do some serious drinking while the owner was absent, catching up on events he had not been in the thick of.

When he returned, eager to learn more from the point of view of a participant in the carnage, Ford explained Edge was his only customer because the majority of his regular patrons were out with the marshal, engaged in the wild goose chase for a woman who was already back in Rikersville. Beyond the reach of the kind of justice the posse was sworn to carry out.

Then, after the saloonkeeper realised Edge was not about to unburden himself of the dark secrets which were making him drink so much so fast, he revealed his own need to talk. Started:

'Seems that breed woman was wanted all over for all kinds of wrongdoin', a lot of it murder. If you're interested?'

'I was real interested, feller,' Edge replied absently, without lifting his gaze from the glass fisted in one hand, the bottle in the other.

Behind his bar, elbows resting on it, his face no longer a mask of misery, Ford failed to read anything into the use of the past tense. And as sounds of Rikersville getting back to some semblance of normality trickled into the saloon from the late afternoon street, he began to eagerly report on events in town since Edge rode out.

'Couple of things happened almost at once. First me lookin' upstairs and findin' Fortune with a knife in him. Then Norris Pascall showin' up in town. He's the Ross county sheriff. Seems the breed woman was mixed up in some plan to rob a timber company payroll wagon that went wrong. Four guys got killed, three of them her partners in the hold up. She didn't get no money off the payroll wagon they held up, but she robbed blind the bodies of her partners: took everythin' off them but the clothes they was wearin'.'

Ford paused and when Edge did not fill it, he said a little apprehensively: 'But I heard tell you already know somethin' of that, mister?'

'Pascall say he was tracking me as well as her?'

Ford shrugged. 'I dunno mister. But most of the talkin' was done between the sheriff from up north and Bernie Brogan. I just heard bits and pieces at second hand. But it seems Pascall got a bunch of flyers on the breed woman. She was wanted all over, for all kindsa stuff. Like I say, some of it killin'.'

'Yeah, you said,' Edge murmured, finished a drink, poured another. Began to roll a new cigarette while one still burned at the side of his mouth.

'Brogan sure said a mouthful about you, mister. When he seen you start to move fast after the breed woman.'

Ford glanced across at Edge, and after he failed to draw a response to this, he screwed up his face in a frown of deep thought: struggled to pick up the threads of his account. Then gave a low grunt when he recalled where he had been before Edge interrupted him with the query.

'Right off after I took him upstairs and he seen what happened to Grant Fortune, Brogan called for volunteer deputies. And along with the Ross sheriff they all set off a runnin' after the breed woman. And you, too, maybe?'

'Maybe,' Edge lit the fresh cigarette from the long butt of the old one.

'Yeah. Well... The dust hadn't hardly settled behind the

153

posse when Rachel Fortune comes back into town from visitin'
with her daughter and that no-account husband of hers.'

'That just your personal opinion?'

'What?'

'Walker being no good?'

'Hell, no! Didn't take long for everybody around Rikersville
to figure out he was that when him and that wife of his squatted
on the piece of land out along the Pacific Road. Said they
planned to farm it, build the best house in this part of the
country on it. Wouldn't listen to what local farmin' folks told
them about how the piece of land they picked flooded in the
winter and took most of spring plantin' time to drain. Then
baked up rock hard in the summer. Some folks, they just won't
listen to good advice.'

'Yeah,' Edge muttered and tried briefly to recall the last time
he took advice. But could not even remember being given any,
unless he counted the message scrawled in the dirt by Ruby
Red. Told himself he should certainly have taken that to heart.

'Grant Fortune knew what kinda son-in-law he had, mister.
Was the third time him and his wife come up from Frisco to
visit with their daughter and the no-account she married. And
them first two times he went away from here a whole lot poorer
than he come. Which was after he staked Walker a time or two
before his daughter even married him, he told me.'

Edge knocked back the latest shot of rye in one, banged the
glass down hard and poured another. And the experienced
saloonkeeper, a veteran of countless across the bar exchanges,
recognised this as a sign that his sole customer was losing
interest in family gossip. He hurried on:

'But that's neither here nor there, I guess. Except it says how
the Walkers were always havin' money problems: which is why
they upped and robbed the bank today?'

He shrugged. 'Every town has it's bad element, and
Rikersville ain't likely to get much of the good any more. New
folks like the Shelby couple, I mean. And I figure they could up
and leave after what happened today. Seems they only brought
the baby into town to see Doc Smith, on account of the little
feller had a fever. And nearly got the baby and themselves shot
just by bein' innocent bystanders.'

154

Ford moved from one end of his counter to the other, lit two kerosene lamps. Then growled 'But hell, that's neither here nor there either. After the posse left in pursuit of the breed woman and you, Rachel Fortune drove back into town on their buggy. Face as long as a country mile from whatever happened out at the Walker place. Big bust-up, I guess, on account of Fortune didn't go along with her, to bankroll Walker some more.

'Then, when she found out he'd been stabbed and robbed by the breed woman, she went cold crazy. If you know what I mean, mister? Like somethin' in her brain snapped. But she didn't rant and rave, stuff like that. You know?'

'Sure, I know,' Edge confirmed.

Ford nodded. 'I guess on top of havin' the big blow up with her daughter and Walker on account of Fortune not visitin'... Then findin' out she'd been right to suspect him of playin' around with the whore of a breed——'

'She wasn't,' Edge cut in.

'What?'

'It was the only thing she cared deeply about, so I figure it was the only subject she didn't lie about. She wasn't a whore.'

Edge was aware he had started to slur some of his words.

Ford said: 'Okay, whatever you say, mister. Whatever it was made her do it, Mrs Fortune wanted her husband buried in double-quick time. She figured the quicker he was put in the ground, the quicker she could start to forget him and the kind of whorin', penny-pinchin' sonofabitch he was. Them are her words, mister.'

Edge poured himself a drink, held up the glass in a gesture that he accepted what the saloonkeeper said.

'And the kind of money she offered—to the undertaker and the preacher and the Widow Edwards for her weeds—well, wasn't no trouble to get the arrangements made quick. Size of the congregation for the service ... Well, I guess folks were just curious to get a close look at the kinda woman who'd do somethin' like that. Bury her husband in such a hurry outta spite.'

He shook his head. 'Me, I'm the only person left in town didn't go to church. Unless you count that poor dumbcluck Erlander girl. I'd been expectin' a rush when the posse showed

155

up. And after the funeral was over I figured some folks would want a drink, wash the taste of what happened outta their mouths. Whatever.

'Them Walkers must've snuck into town real quiet. Busted into the bank out back. I sure enough never knew they were anyplace close by until I seen them bust outta the bank. After I seen you and the breed woman come back to town, climb up on my balcony. But I guess they knew more about the bank than most hereabouts. Apart from old man Lovell that runs it. Been in there often enough, dickerin' for loans and hardly ever gettin' one. About covers it, mister.'

'I'm obliged,' Edge said.

'And the town oughta be obliged to you. If you hadn't plugged Dan Walker when you did, he'd have killed Clarice Erlander. That was plain to see. And who knows who else?'

'I sure wouldn't, feller,' Edge said, making an effort not to slur. Then he carefully replaced the cork in the neck of the bottle. 'But I don't know much about anything. Maybe I will when I get older.'

'Uh?' Ford expressed nervousness as he watched Edge get to his feet, knock back a final shot of whiskey and bring the bottle to the bar.

'How much I owe?'

Ford adamantly shook his head. 'On the house, mister. Clarice Erlander didn't deserve to lose her daughter that way, and the way you kept her from bein'——'

Edge had stooped to squint at the bottle, judge the level left in it. Then he took out his roll, peeled off two dollar bills and placed them on the bartop. 'Always pay my way.'

Ford looked unhappy, but offered no argument.

Edge glimpsed his reflection in the mottled and dusty mirror behind the bar, then caught an image of the table where he had seen Ruby Red with the man she was later to kill for no other reason than money. He peered again at his own lopsided expression, and thought about the strange look that had been on his face, the look that had caused Ruby Red to stare at him with such intensity just before she took the two bullets that killed her. And he abruptly recalled that the last time he had felt such an expression take control of his features was up in the

Dakotas. When he was with Beth and——'

'You okay, mister?'

'Uh?' Edge shook his head violently to rid his mind of memories he did not want to recall in relation to a woman like Ruby Red.

'You looked kinda strange there for awhile, mister,' Ford explained apprehensively. 'Not like a ... Hell, there was almost a wild animal look about you. If you don't mind me sayin' so?'

'No sweat,' Edge answered. He turned away from the bar, took considerable trouble to put one foot carefully in front of the other so he could walk to the batwing doors without bumping into tables and chairs. 'Guess it's lucky I didn't go ape.'

'What?'

Edge pushed out between the doors, said to the empty, night-shrouded street: 'Seeing as how somebody made a monkey out of me.'

EDGE 59: TERROR TOWN

GEORGE G. GILMAN

Up to now the good people of Winton, Oregon had done a lot of things right. The town was prosperous, the buildings well constructed and in a good state of repair. The law was upheld and all seemed orderly. The elderly judge was eloquent in his praise for the respectable nature of the citizens.

Trouble was, just before the man called Edge rode in to town, things had started to go all wrong. A woman had been brutally murdered and a man hurriedly tried and hanged. The wrong man.

And now a person or persons unknown had set up a protest movement. Not by waving banners but by setting up nooses. And beginning to kill, one by one, all the people responsible.

That was when bad law became lynch law and the formerly neatly swept streets became all littered with the bodies of those recently responsible people.

MORE GREAT WESTERN READING
FROM GEORGE G. GILMAN

THE EDGE SERIES

- ☐ 05543 3 Edge 43: Arapaho Revenge £1.00
- ☐ 05901 4 Edge 51: A Time For Killing £1.50
- ☐ 41381 0 Edge 56: Doom Town £1.95
- ☐ 42245 3 Edge 57: Dying Is Forever £1.95
- ☐ 42409 X Edge 58: The Desperadoes £1.95
- ☐ 43110 X Edge 59: Terror Town £1.99

THE STEELE SERIES

- ☐ 30935 7 Steele 41: The Killing Strain £1.50
- ☐ 40228 2 Steele 42: The Big Gunfight £1.95
- ☐ 40846 9 Steele 43: The Hunted £1.95
- ☐ 41734 4 Steele 45: The Outcasts £1.95
- ☐ 42269 0 Steele 46: The Return £1.95
- ☐ 42852 4 Steele 47: Trouble In Paradise..... £1.95
- ☐ 48775 X Steele 48: Going Back £1.99

All these books are available at your local bookshop or newsagent, or can be ordered direct from the publisher. Just tick the titles you want and fill in the form below.

Prices and availability subject to change without notice.

HODDER AND STOUGHTON PAPERBACKS, P.O. Box 11, Falmouth, Cornwall.

Please send cheque or postal order, and allow the following for postage and packing:

U.K. – 55p for one book, plus 22p for the second book, and 14p for each additional book ordered up to a £1.75 maximum.

B.F.P.O. and EIRE – 55p for the first book, plus 22p for the second book, and 14p per copy for the next 7 books, 8p per book thereafter.

OTHER OVERSEAS CUSTOMERS – £1.00 for the first book, plus 25p per copy for each additional book.

Name ....

Address ....

....